The
Wheels
Turn

2

Chapter 1

As I shook the feather mattress I could hear my friends playing outside. I was seven years old and there was always housework to do when I arrived home from school. Mary Ashton came to call for me every day, but I don't know why she bothered, because by the time I had finished my jobs it was getting dark and it was too late to go out to play. My Grandma used to go to the door and tell my friends to clear off and then she would sit back down in her rocking chair, reading her rubbish love stories, which she picked up from the library every week. Yes, Grandma was never happy unless she was sitting reading and eating chocolate which she kept in her apron pocket, which was all she did every day. I could hear my friends with their skipping ropes and the squeals of laughter rose up with the chanting of their skipping rhymes. Mother would come in at six o'clock every evening and start preparing our meal, which consisted of a bowl of broth and chunks of bread. Mother would pick up bones from the butcher every Saturday morning, Mr Jackson, the butcher, made sure there were still bits of meat attached to them. She would boil them in a big black saucepan on the fire and add a few carrots, turnips, and potatoes. This is what we ate every day and we had bread and dripping for breakfast. Before dad was killed our meals were very different, we would eat a joint of meat at the weekends and lovely pies and puddings throughout the week. Mother was a very good cook, but this all changed after I lost my dad. She worked from six o'clock every morning at the washhouse down the road and, after tea she dragged her weary body to scrub the floors at the nearby hospital. I finished making the beds and then swept up the dust, we only had lino on the floors and the dust from the beds made so much mess. Grandma called up the stairs, "Get a move on young lady, I want a cup of tea," so I left off what I was doing and went downstairs and filled the heavy kettle with water and set it on the fire. If I didn't do things straight away I got a clout across the head and even if I did, I still got a clout. Grandma seemed to enjoy hitting me, but by now I had come to accept it, at one time I would try to dodge out of her way, now I just stood there and let her hit me. She was such an awful old lady and every night I prayed that she would die and my Grandma Clayton would come to live with us. Grandma Clayton was my favourite person in the whole world, although she lived at the other side of our village, and I didn't see her very often, she always gave me a big hug and there was always a bar of chocolate for me in her sideboard cupboard. Grandma Clayton was my dad's mother and she had brought up her family of eight boys with love and kindness. Grandad Clayton had been killed in the pit along with my dad and one of his brothers, but the light still shone in Grandma's eyes as she struggled each day to look after her family.

When I was seven years old my dad was killed in the pit, but I do remember him so well. He always seemed to be at work and when he did come home he was very tired. Mum would bring the old tin bath up the cellar steps and set the copper in the corner to boil so there would be plenty of hot water for his bath. As he came through the back door he would take off his clothes covered with the coal dust and get into the bath in the front of the fireplace, and mum would stoke up the fire and back it up with coal so the room would be nice and warm. His towels were laid over the fireguard and mum would scrub his back. My Grandma still sat in her old rocking chair muttering to herself that her tea wasn't ready, whilst I danced around with dad splashing water on me. Yes, those days were very happy but mother was a different person to the one she is today. She used to sit me on her knee in front of the fire and tell me stories, which she made up as she went along. She was good at telling stories was my mum, and I didn't know it, but she was also expecting my baby brother or sister.

All this came to an end the night of February 11th 1937, everyone in our village was woken to the sound of the pit disaster hooter blowing at four-fifteen in the morning. All the women whose men folk were down the pit, rushed to the pithead to find out what was happening. Mother lifted me from my bed and wrapped me in a blanket and we ran in the darkness to take up our positions as near to the winding wheels as we could. Grandma followed on behind moaning and grumbling because she had been disturbed. Grandad Pointer had died from tuberculosis earlier that year and she knew his illness was from breathing in the coal dust whilst working underground. As mother stood with the other women the news was beginning to leak out. The old deep mine workings were blocked by a fall of earth and sixteen men were trapped. The women collected together with their shawls wrapped tightly round their heads to keep out the bitter cold. "What have you brought the bairn for?" asked Lily Pursehouse. "I need her with me," replied my mother. "It ain't seem right bringing a bairn out in this weather," she said, "you know they'll all be dead." "Stop this kind of talk," said my Grandma, "it won't help any of us." "What's happening?" called Lily Pursehouse as the men congregated at the pithead. Ambulances had started to arrive and the winding wheels were turning. Men were climbing out of the pit cage their faces grim and set. The moaning and crying from the women fell into the night air. "Not much hope lass," remarked one miner as his blackened streaked face looked up to the sky as he gave thanks for his life.

As daylight dawned, an eerie quietness hung over the scene, the crying, and wailing from the women had stopped. They were all too tired and weary to take in what was happening, but still they stood with their heads bent low. The only news they received were the names of the men who were trapped. Their names had been hurriedly written on a scrap of paper by one of the rescuers and pinned upon a post, and three of those names were my dad, Jim Clayton, his father Joseph and his brother Arthur. This was a tragedy beyond all magnitude and when my Grandma Clayton joined us at the pit top her face was full of the most horrendous grief. She took me from my mother's arms and sat on the nearest boulder swinging her body too and fro in her pain. As morning broke the rescuers were still toiling away underground trying to reach the trapped men. The women had started to disperse when they knew their men folk were safe. My Grandma Pointer wanted to take me home, but mother wouldn't hear of it and I can remember waking up and peeping out from my blanket and wondering what was happening. Mother assured me there was nothing to worry about so I snuggled back down to my Grandma Clayton's warm breast. Hot sweet tea was passed around and I was given a drink, which warmed my tummy.

"Take the bairn home," yelled Ted Hinchcliffe, one of the overseers at the pit, "things are going to get grim very soon and we don't want her upset." Grandma Pointer whisked me from my lovely warm spot and we trudged back to our house. It was mid day before mother came home and still there was no news of my dad, she looked so tired and wan when she came through the door. She picked me up and held me close and we both cried together. I remember that day although I was only tiny. Grandma Clayton had gone back home to her brood and now all we could do was wait.

Mother rinsed her face and then gave me a bowl of broth. "Where's mine?" snapped Grandma Pointer. "Can't you get it yourself?" replied my mother. I had never heard her answer her back before, and my Grandma grudgingly got out of her chair and filled herself a bowl. "Aren't you having some?" said Grandma. "I'm not hungry," said mother. "What about your bairn?" said Grandma, "that'll need some nourishment." Mother turned away as her tired eyes brimmed with tears. "Crying ain't going to bring him back," said Grandma. "Oh mother won't you shut up," replied my mother. "Don't speak to me like that young lady," replied Grandma, "it might be better if your kid dies anyway, when you're on your own you'll have enough mouths to feed." Mother's sobbing heaved at her body. I tried to put my arms around her but she didn't seem to want me near. She wanted to go back to the pithead but had been advised by Tom Bratley, the rescue leader, that they would let her know when there was some news.

Chapter 2

Tom Bratley surveyed the scene before him, and lifted his mask from around his mouth and spoke to the team of rescuers waiting for his instructions. He knew the seam where the men were trapped, it was one of the deepest and most fearful places to be. He talked things through with his deputy, Sam Johnson, an old hand at rescue work. He had worked in the mines for almost forty years starting when he was eleven years old, there was nothing he hadn't come across, and his tired face and bent body showed a man worn out and old before his time.

The men were given their orders and the digging and shoring began. Volunteers out numbered the pit rescue team and in silence they worked. All that could be heard were the picks and shovels and the orders from the man in charge. It was agreed a tunnel would be dug for one man to crawl through. They shored up the roof and sides as they went along and the men worked in teams so that when their arms and backs were tired from the gruelling work, they could have a rest. Right through the day the men toiled only to be relieved by a new set of volunteers. Tom Bratley knew how easily the water could seep in and his main fear was the sound of a deluge sweeping through and drowning the trapped men and also the lives of the rescuers.

The men did not speak, each one knew of the perils they faced. They wiped their fevered brows and tried not to think of the outcome. Most of them knew the news would probably be bad, but still they toiled on. They inched their way nearer but the movement was slow, the only sounds to be heard were the picks and shovels biting into the fallen rock. The air was stale and dank and the men were gasping for breath. Water dripped down the walls of the pit as the weary men battled on. "Can't you work faster," demanded Tom Bratley, knowing only too well that the men were working their hearts out. "Go easy on them Tom," said Sam Johnson. "Aye tha rait, I'm just getting frustrated," replied Tom, "you've got to admit this ones a bad un though."

The time passed slowly, but suddenly he heard the sound of water trickling through the existing walls. It swirled around the men's boots and a feeling of panic prevailed but still the men worked on. Tom Bratley waded through the water still urging the rescuers to keep going. His turn came and he dug out the debris with all his might adjusting his oxygen mask as he battled on. Suddenly he heard a sound. Knock, knock, knock. "Quiet men," he yelled, "listen I hear knocking." There came a deathly hush and there it was again, knock, knock, knock. "We must be near," he exclaimed, "they must be still alive." There was a cheer from the weary workers as old Sam knocked back on the solid coal. Knock, knock, knock. For a while there was silence and then again the faint knocking sound was heard. Bill Coombes was next in line and as he climbed back into the tunnel his weary soaking body had new purpose. Tom Bratley sent a message back along the line to the waiting men and soon the news was taken to the wives back home.

Seeing Arnold Batty coming through our gate, mother raced to the door, her face distorted and tired. "Good news lass," said Arnold, "sounds have been heard, we think the men may still be alive." Mother put her shawl around her shoulders. "Look after Annie for me please," she asked Grandma Pointer. To which she just grunted. "Can't I come with you?" I asked. "Best not love," replied Arnold Batty, "its bitter cold out there, you'd better stay at side o'fire." Mother gave me a hug and made me promise to be a good girl, and off she went. By now the men were feverishly working in the tunnel. "Don't take any risks," yelled Tom Bratley, "you ain't shoring it up properly." The water continued to seep in, by now they were up to their knees. Every few minutes they stopped to listen but the knocking had stopped. Fearing for the rescuers safety, Tom Bratley called a halt to the working. "Gather round me men," he called, "I'm giving you a choice, conditions are getting worse, the water is rising and I don't think there is much hope for the trapped men, if you want to get out now, do so and no worse will be thought of you." The men look from one to another and a mumbled discussion took place. Without hesitation unanimous agreement was reached, they would carry on. Mustering as much strength as they could manage, the routine began again. Albert Mason was the first to enter the tunnel, the roof was beginning to creak. "Shore it up more, if you have any doubts," yelled Tom Bratley, "safety is more important than time."

Gradually Albert inched his way ahead when suddenly he heard a moan. Sticking out of the rubble was a man's foot. Albert let out a yell. "I need help," he called, "someone come and join me." Tom Bratley crawled on his hands and knees to join Albert. "What's a miss lad?" said Tom as he squeezed his soaking body to the side of Albert Mason. "Look what I have found," said Albert, "listen to the moaning, he's still alive Tom." With their hands they clawed at the rubble, carefully scraping the dirt away from the man's inert body. There was space for them to move and it was obvious the small area where the man laid the roof had held up, so he was at least able to breath. "Shine your lamp on his face," yelled Tom, "lets free his air passages." Albert stretched over and the man let out a yell. "He's badly injured," said Albert, "we need to get him out." "Call for backup," said Tom. Albert crawled back through the tunnel and shouted for assistance. "Get a stretcher and bring it through, we have found one man." With careful manoeuvring, the stretcher was manhandled through the tunnel. "Careful now lads," said Tom, as they gently lifted the injured man. "Ease him carefully," said Albert, as their gnarled strong hands lifted him on to the stretcher. The man moaned in pain and somehow he was taken back along the shored up tunnel and onto the waiting pit cage. "Can tha see who it is?" said Ernie Davenport, "clear the muck from round his face." "It's Jed Harper," replied Albert. "By gum he's lucky," said Ernie. An air of relief swept through the men, and as the stretcher was taken away a new lot of volunteers arrived to carry on with the digging.

At the top of the pit shaft, the wives stood waiting. Betty Harper, her heavily pregnant body, leaned over and saw the face on the stretcher." "It's my Jed," she cried, as her body keeled over as pain shot through her belly. The women gathered round her. This was her fifth baby, and she knew she wouldn't make it home. "My baby's coming," she screamed. "Take her t'pit office," said Mary Crabtree. Between them they lifted and dragged her along as the ambulance took her Jed to the local hospital. Carefully the women laid her on a blanket on the floor, and Mary Crabtree knelt by her side. The baby's head had now appeared and Betty Harper screamed with pain. "Keep pushing," said Mary, "your baby is here, you've got another lad." Betty let out a moan, not another lad, she said to herself, as she heard the baby cry. Oh! How she had prayed for a girl. All her lads would finish up down the pit. But right now she felt too weak to be bothered. Mary Crabtree wrapped the little lad in her shawl and did her best to clear up the mess. "Come on now Betty, you've got to suckle this youngster," said Mary. "But I can hardly lift my head up," said Betty. "Here lass I'll help you," said Maria Clayton, "thas had a real shock," and carefully she put her arms around this poor woman and eased her gently into a sitting position. The baby was put to her breast and Betty cuddled him, whilst tears of relief ran down her cheeks. "This baby wasn't due for another month," she said. "He's a big un," replied Mary Crabtree, "and looks healthy enough, and by the way he yells, he's got good lungs on him." "Pity he'll finish up down't pit, getting em filled with coal dust," said Annie Pritchard. "I don't know how thas going to cope wi your Jed all smashed up, looks like he's brocken every bone in his body to my way of thinking," she added. "Lets not have any more of that talk Annie," replied Mary Crabtree, "once they get him to hospital and clean him up he will be alright." "Wouldn't put too much hope on that." said Annie, "poor buggar looked de'ad to me, God help thee if thas got to bring that brood up on thee own." Betty Harper started to cry and passed the baby to Maria Clayton. "Here you take him," she said, "I'm having all on holding him," and she flopped back down on the floor with sheer exhaustion. "Come on let's get her back home," said Mary Crabtree, when suddenly Charlie Price popped his head round the door. "Are you alright in here," he said. Mary Crabtree took control. "Betty's had her baby," she said, "we need to get her home, can some of you men come and carry her." "Aye missus, just give mi a minute and I'll get some of the lads, trouble is it's started snowing so we will have to go careful." "Right," said Mary, "let's get you and your bairn wrapped up and ready for home, the men will be here in a minute." Maria Clayton put her hand on her belly, she felt her baby move, and she was very frightened. The men arrived and young Andy Purshouse tried to make a joke about first being at a pit rescue and then having to rescue a mother and new baby, but it all fell on deaf ears. They scooped up Betty Harper like a sack of coal and one man tucked the baby under his coat and they set off for home. The rest of the women returned to the pithead.

Chapter 3

The men underground resumed their digging. The slight ray of hope they had when they found Jed Harper dropped to misery and despair as they toiled at the hard rock. Their weary faces showed of their anguish. "Keep at it lads," said Tom Bratley, trying to urge them on. "Don't you think you should have a break," said Harry Parker, "you've been down here nearly twelve hours already." "I'm alright," he replied, "I must see this through." Then there was a shout at the end of the tunnel, cowering in the deep water were the trapped men. Sam Johnson had found them, two were floating on the surface, and the rest had been drowned, trapped by the boulders that held them down. Sam shouted to Tom Bratley, "We got here too late Tom, they are all dead." Tom viewed the scene from the light of his helmet and told his men to return to the pit cage ready to go back up to the surface. They made their way through the slimy water, half swimming, half walking. No one spoke. Gradually the pit wheels wound them back to the top. As they climbed out of the cage the waiting women surged forward for news. Tom Bratley step forward and spoke to Harry White, the pit manager, who was waiting with the women. They were all huddled together, their frozen bodies tired and worn. They watched as Harry White walked across to them. "The news is not good I'm afraid," he said, "I'm sorry but all your men have drowned at the pit bottom, I am so very sorry." The women clung together for support and their wailing went up into the snow driven sky. "May God help you all," he said as his voice vanished into the cold air.

The women split up and trundled back home. Maria Clayton just managed to reach the back door when she collapsed. "What's wrong with you, our Maria," said her mother and pushed me out of the way. "Oh My God!" said grandma, "go and fetch Ivy Parsons straight away," and gave me a smack across my head. I ran to the Parson's house as fast as my legs could carry me. "Come quickly," I said to Mrs Parsons. "What's up?" she said, "can't you see I'm just having me tea." "It's my mother," I said, "she's fallen on the floor." "Alright luv I'll come over, get yourself back home and tell them I won't be long." I ran back home and mother had gone to bed, I could hear her screaming. Ivy Parsons followed me in and knocked the snow off her boots and went up stairs. Grandma came down and fetched the kettle off the fire. "Boil some more water in't pan," said Grandma, "and be quick about it." I lifted the saucepan off the shelf and filled it with water and as Grandma went past me she scuffed me round the head. I could hear mother moaning up stairs and I felt very frightened. I went and sat on the bottom stair, I didn't know what to do with myself. They all seemed to have forgotten I existed. So I hummed a little tune to myself and waited. "I stood beside a brooklet that sparkled on its way," I sang. This was a lovely song we sang at school, and although I couldn't read properly, I knew all the words to this song about a trout playing in the water. Suddenly I heard Ivy Parsons say, "It was a little lad," to my Grandma. I didn't know what she meant so I carried on singing. Grandma came down the stairs and cuffed me round the head. "Less of that cat-a-whaling," she said, "your mother doesn't want to hear that row and shift yourself off the stairs." "What's wrong with my mum?" I said. "Now't to do wi you," said Grandma. "When will my dad be home?" I carried on. "Seen the last of him you have, got his sen trapped in't pit the silly fool." I didn't know what to do so I just cried at the thought of not seeing my dad again. "Crying in't going to bring him back so shut up and put kettle on." She settled herself in her rocking chair, picked up her book and started to read with her mouth full of chocolate. Ivy Parsons came downstairs, "I've cleaned her up best I can," she said to Grandma, "I'll put all the rubbish in't bin on my way home." Grandma didn't answer and Ivy Parsons went to the door. Not to be put off I went over to the door before she had chance to get outside. "What's wrong wi me mum?" I asked again. "She's alright love, just a bit upset that's all, she having a little sleep so just leave her alone for an hour or two." As she opened the door an icy blast blew in followed by a swirl of snow. "Thank you for coming," I said, although I didn't know what she had been for.

Chapter 4

The surgeon looked up from the operating table. "Nothing more we can do for him I'm afraid," he said, "it's up to the faith in God whether he pulls through or not." So slowly Jed Harper was wheeled into a room where he would not be disturbed. The nurses settled him in and adjusted his drips and heart monitor. There was coal dust still ingrained in his tired waxen face. "Might as well be dead as be in the mess he's in," said Nurse Carter. "You know what they say, while there's life there's hope," replied Sister Doherty, a fine looking nurse from Ireland. "We must keep an extra close eye on him, the next few hours are vital." "I'll sit with him for a while just in case." She pulled her chair close to the man's bed and gently took his gnarled hand in hers. She hummed softly under her breath, "Oh Danny boy the pipes the pipes are calling, from glen to glen and down the mountainside." She gazed at the man's face, he was a good-looking guy and could not be much more than thirty years old. After an hour had passed she gently let go of his hand and went about her duties. "Wonder if we shall get any more of them in?" said Nurse Carter. "We shall just have to wait and see," said Sister Doherty.

The weary rescuers returned to their homes, worn out and troubled with leaden hearts. The sharp north wind cut through their tired bodies as the snow swirled round their heads. "You did your best lads," said Tom Bratley, "don't be too down, it wasn't meant to be." Meanwhile the recovery men had taken over and inch by inch the poor men's bodies were gently lifted along the make shift tunnel. Slowly they were brought to the surface and whisked away in the waiting ambulances. "Straight to the morgue we'll take them, shall we?" remarked one driver. "No they've got to go to the hospital first," said Joe Simmonite. So the journey began. Waiting for the men to arrive was Alan Hodkin, the chief registrar at the hospital. As each body was laid in their respective places the doctor in charge examined the poor men. Most of the men hadn't a mark on them and looked as though they were asleep. The women were kept away from the pit, but by now they all knew the fate of their men folk.

Sister Doherty was due to go off duty but felt she must take one last look at Jed Harper before she went home. I'll stay with him for a while, she said to herself. So once more she took hold of his hand and gently hummed a little tune. She could feel her head getting heavy and her eyes began to close. Better go home, she thought to herself and she carefully put his hand back under the sheet and said a little prayer for him. Why she should take such an interest in this man she would never know, but her heart went out to him. Next day she arrived at the hospital and took over from Sister Newby. "What's new today?" she said as brightly as she could muster. "We lost Mr Harper in the night," said Sister Newby, "the poor man didn't stand much chance." Sister Doherty caught her breath and turned her head so no one could see the tears roll down her cheeks.

Chapter 5

Mother got up next day, she looked dazed and tired. "Mum, what's wrong?" I asked. "Nothing love, I'm just a bit off colour, that's all," she replied. "Why isn't my dad coming home?" I asked. "I've told her he's been killed in't pit," said my Grandma. "Oh! Don't be so cruel mother, she's only a bairn," said my mother. "But she's got to know," said Grandma, "he ain't suddenly going to walk through dooer." Mother started to cry and huge sobs shook her body. I went across and sat on her knee and we cried together. She stroked my brow and said, "There's only you and me now Annie we've got to help each other." "What about me?" said Grandma. "Oh! you always think of yourself don't you," said mother, "from now on things will have to change so I'll need more help from you." The days passed by and arrangements were made for the men to be buried. I'd never been to a funeral before and Grandma wanted me to go next door to stay with Mrs Sutton but my mum wanted me there. Mrs Sutton was a nice lady and they only had one son, Harold, who was two years older than me. Mr Sutton worked in the pit office doing the men's wages. He was a cashier or something. They brought my dad home and he was laid out in the front room. No one was allowed in our front room, only on Sundays when mother lit the fire and we went to sit in there. We had a horsehair settee with a drop end and two chairs in dark green and they were kept covered up all week. We also had a sideboard on which stood the family photos and a big plant called an Aspidistra, I think. All the neighbours came in to see my dad and mum sat by the side of his coffin as if in a trance. On the second day he was at home mother took me by the hand and led me into the front room. "Come on now Annie," she said, " come and say goodbye to your dad." "You're not taking her in there our Maria are you?" said Grandma. "Why not?" said mother. "Cos she's only little," said Grandma. "I want her to see him for the very last time," said mother. "Well don't cry to me when she has nightmares," said Grandma. I didn't know what a nightmare was, so I wasn't worried and I took hold of mother's hand and went into the front room. The curtains were drawn and I could hardly see. "Just a minute Annie," said mother, "I will light the gas mantle." Mother struck a match and the mantle popped and a soft grey light fell over the room. All I could see was my dad's face. He was all covered in silk and what I couldn't understand, he had two pennies on his eyes. "Mum, he just looks fast asleep," I said. "Yes he does love,"replied mother, "but just say goodbye to him and tell him how you feel." I leaned over the coffin and whispered, "Goodbye dad, I will always love you," and I reached out and touched him gently on his face. Mother was crying as she led me out of the room, pulling the gas light cord as she passed. "You'll be happy now our Maria," said Grandma, "I think thas teckon leave of thee senses."

The next day was the funeral. The snow was still thick on the ground and as we followed the hearse I had to cling onto my mother as I kept slipping. Grandma trudged along grumbling and groaning about how we would all catch our death of cold. My dad's funeral was the fourth to be held out of the sixteen. All the bosses from the pit were there and Mr White, the pit manager. I don't remember much about the service but as I watched my dad's coffin being lowered into the grave, I made up my mind I would always come and visit him as long as I lived.

Chapter 6

Betty Harper had not been strong enough to go and see her husband whilst he was in hospital and she'd only been able to find out how he was from old Ben Cox her next-door neighbour who had been round to see him. Ben came to see her and said he was alright, so Betty put the baby to bed and prayed for her man. "Gather round me lads," she said to her five sons, "let's sit and pray for your dad's recovery." The baby was asleep in his wicker basket in front of the fire. The boys stopped what they were doing. Jed, the eldest was eight and in the year above me at school, Jacky was seven and in my class. I didn't like Jacky, he didn't have the same good looks as his brother Jed, and he used to torment me and pull my hair. Billy was five and half and had only just started school, he was a nice looking boy but always seemed to cry a lot. I didn't know the youngest two very well, Sidney was four and Alec two and half. I felt sorry for Betty Harper she always looked tired and harassed, and now she had another baby to look after. I prayed at night for Mr Harper to get better.

Betty sat in the battered old armchair passed on from her mother, and gathered the boys around her. She reached out for the little ones and together they prayed for their father. Betty had known Jed Harper all her life, they went to the same school together, and she'd always admired this strong healthy young man who was always there for her. They walked home from school together and he would pull her leg about her freckles and ginger hair but as she grew older she blossomed into a beautiful young lady with lovely auburn tresses and they soon fell in love. By the time she was sixteen she was pregnant with Jed junior and a hurried wedding was arranged. At first they lived with Jed's mother and father, Jed had worked down the pit since he was eleven. When they got their own pit house they quickly moved in with their new baby. Jed's mother Gertie and his dad Jed were glad to see them go because really there wasn't enough room for them. They had five other children to consider and Betty and Jed had to sleep in the front room.

Life was so much better when they were on their own. They managed to furnish one room and Betty's mother gave them a bed and wardrobe, and although they had a struggle to keep going they were so much happier to be in their own little house.

Now here she was with six little boys and her man badly injured lying prostrate in a hospital bed. God give me strength to keep going, she prayed, and dreaded the sound of the knock on the door telling her that her Jed had passed away.

"Will dad be coming home soon?" said Jed, the wisest eight years old you could ever wish to meet. "Let's hope so son," said Betty. "I'll help you look after him," he said, and she knew he meant it. "Come on now, off to school with you," she said. "But can't I stop at home with you," asked Jed. "No, my lad you're better off at school," she said, as she reached down their coats from the high pegs and saw them off at the door. "Come straight home," she said, "no going down't meadows." She knew she could trust Jed, but Billy and Jacky often wandered down on to the meadows where the stream ran with full force. It was a game the kids played to see who could jump across the stream as a dare, but some times the water was deep and flowed in full spate down to the river. The kids were warned at school about keeping away from the meadows but they never took any notice.

Betty turned her thoughts to what she had to do. The baby was crying and needed feeding and the other two wanted breakfast. She filled up two bowls from the porringer and sat the children to the table. "Get on with your porridge, that's good boys," she said, and picked up the baby and held him to her breast. She stared into the fire and thought of her Jed. She would try to go to see him today, she thought. But she knew she couldn't take her bairns out in this terrible weather, but who would look after them for her. Suddenly her thoughts were disturbed by a knock on the door. Who can this be at this time, she said to herself. Covering her swollen breast she went to the door. Standing there in the thick snow was Tom Bratley. "Come in Tom," said Betty, "what are you here for on such a nasty day." "I'm afraid it's bad news Betty lass, thas lost your Jed." "Oh no!" screamed Betty as her legs buckled beneath her as she fell to the floor. Tom Bratley caught the baby and laid him in his basket. He bent over Betty and lifted her into the chair, he gave her a drink of water and slowly the colour returned to her cheeks. "Tell me he hasn't gone," she murmered. "Sorry lass, it happened for't best, he was very badly injured." "But what am I going to do now?" she said, as the waves of nausea gripped her body. The children sat quietly at the table. "I don't know lass," said Tom, "but I'll have to go home now, I'm on afters and I ain't got much time, shall I fetch thee somebody before I go?" "No, I'll be alright Tom," said Betty, "you get off and thanks for coming." Tom buttoned up his coat and put his cap firmly back on his head and went to the back door. "Are tha sure tha'll be alright lass," he said, and with a deep sigh he was gone.

Betty walked slowly to the sink, dumped the empty porridge dishes in the bowl and sat in the worn out armchair. Clutching her boys round her she sobbed till her heart would break. The two little fellows clung to their mother so very bewildered. But Betty was made from sterner stuff, there and then she knew she would fight to survive no matter what happened in her world. Yes! she would miss her Jed and yes she would be lonely, but her boys would now be her life, and, although she knew she would have to struggle, somehow she would survive.

Chapter 7

The day after my dad's funeral was to be the worst day of all especially for my Grandma Clayton. She had been at my dad's funeral and I had never known her be so subdued, but today she was burying her husband, my dear old Grandad, Jim Clayton and my Uncle Arthur, dad's brother. My Grandad had spent most of his life down the pit and was only fifty eight when he was killed. I didn't know him very well but when I did see him, he made such an impression on me with his stories and knowledge. He occasionally met me out of school when he was on the night shift. We would walk together and he would hold my hand as we walked along. My little hand enveloped in his big strong wrinkled one. We always called at Dalton's, the sweet shop, I used to stand with my nose pressed to the window wondering what to have. The big jars were lined up full of everything you fancied from dolly mixtures to humbugs and every make of sweets you could mention. He would say, "Come on now our Annie, make your mind up," and I would go in and choose and come out with my paper coned shaped bag full to the brim. I always thought that Mr Dalton put a few more in mine than anybody elses. Then we would set off for home and I would listen to his stories. He always made me laugh and now at seven years old, I realised, I would never see him again. The night before the funeral we had just said 'Goodbye' to the last of the relatives who had been to Dad's funeral. They had all come back to our house for a sandwich and a cup of tea, when Grandma Pointer announced she was not going to the funeral tomorrow. "Why not?" said my mother who was still in shock. "Well I've had enough," she said, "and no one will miss me." "Don't you think I might need you there," said mother. "Tha dun't need me," said Grandma, "but if tha likes tha can leave young Annie wi me." Mother shook her head in disbelief, "You are a selfish person," she said, and went upstairs out of the way. I followed her and she was sitting on the bed stroking her brow. "What's wrong mum," I said. "Nothing love," she replied, "but come here and sit beside me." I plonked myself on the bed on top of the big comfy eiderdown and my mum put her arms around me and there we sat and neither of us spoke. After a while my mum spoke gently to me, "there's only you and me now Annie, we shall have to help one another get through this," she said. "I'll help you as much as I can," I replied, " but what about Grandma Pointer?" "Oh, she's just a selfish old lady, all she thinks about is herself and her library books and chocolate, try not to take too much notice of her because all she will do is upset you." We walked downstairs together and as we came into the living room Grandma said, "What have you been doing you two behind my back, can't you see it needs some coal on't fire and where's me tea?" Mother picked up the coal bucket and threw the coal on the back of the fire. "Do you think you could go and fill the bucket up before it gets dark?" she said to me. So off I went down the yard slipping and sliding on the frozen snow. I filled up the bucket tried to lift it. I realised it was too heavy so I picked off the biggest lumps and threw them back into the coal shed. I struggled with the heavy bucket and managed to lift it up the back steps. "Look here our Maria she's only brought half a bucket, that'll not go far," said my Grandma as she cuffed me across the head. "She couldn't carry anymore, could you love?" said mother, "and stop hitting her." "Needs a few more good hidings to my way of thinking," said Grandma and went back to her book. I think my mother was too tired to argue any more. We sat down to a bowl of broth and a bit of boiled ham in sandwiches left over from the funeral tea. "Is this all we're having," said Grandma, "I'm hungry." "Make the most of it," said mother, "I don't know how we're going to manage from now on." When I went to bed that night I thought that today had been the most awful day of my life and swore that when I grew up I would try to make life easier for my mother and made up my mind never to marry a miner, life was just too hard.

Chapter 8

If I thought yesterday had been a bad day, I hadn't realised that today would be far worse. We got up to more snow and when we set off to Grandmas house we were wet through by the time we got there. I decided to go with mother, anything was better than staying with Grandma Pointer. I think mother was glad to have me there and she held my hand tightly as we tramped along through the freshly fallen snow. We walked behind the coffins on their horse driven carts. The church was packed once more with all the miners and their families. I sat with mother and Grandma, and Aunty Hilda (Uncle Arthur's wife) sat at the front. With them were my other uncles, (dad's brothers) and my cousins Johnny, Herbert and Wilfred. They were all crying so I thought I'd better cry as well, but somehow I had no tears left. I looked at my mother's face at the side of me and she looked so forlorn. We all stood round the graves, which were right next to my dad's. Dad's grave looked so lonely, covered in snow and with just one bunch of flowers on the top. While no one was looking I wandered over to my dad's grave, I bent over and touched the petals and brushed off the snow and said, in a very quiet voice, "I love you dad." When I returned to the others, no one knew I'd been missing and somehow I felt much better. We all trooped back to my Grandmas and tried to get warm in front of the fire. We had boiled ham sandwiches and tea, I sat next to my cousin Wilfred. He usually tormented me and I didn't like him, but today he never spoke to me. When we got home that night mother fetched the bath up the cellar and I had a nice warm bath in front of the fire. "What are you bathing her today for?" said Grandma, "you know Friday night is bath night and you've used all the water out of the copper." "I'm going in as well," said mother, "we need a hot bath after what we've been through today," and she undressed her weary body and climbed in the water after me. I stood in front of the fire with the threadbare towel round me. "Can't you dry her for me," said mother. "She's big enough to dry her sen," said Grandma and carried on reading.

Chapter 9

The days passed slowly as everyone tried to get back to normal again. Slowly the snow vanished and the first signs of Spring began to show. Mother went for a job at the washhouse and I moved up to the big school just after my eighth birthday. When I got up for school in a morning mother had already gone to work and she used to leave my clothes laid out on the bed for me. I helped myself to porridge out of the porringer and shouted tara to Grandma, who was still in bed, as I went out through the back door. I always met Mary Ashton at the end of our entry and we would walk to school together. She was in the same class as me and we were inseparable. We were both in Miss Dakin's class and she was a lovely teacher. I always did well in my lessons and loved learning. My cousin, Wilfred was in my class and he always used to call me names when we were in the playground. He said I was teacher's pet, which made me cry. One day he pinched my skipping rope and threw it over the wall into the field and I couldn't get it back, but Jed Harper saw him do it and he climbed over the wall to fetch it for me. I liked Jed Harper and I knew he had a lot on at home helping his mother and all the boys. He was very good looking with lovely dark wavy hair. All the girls liked him. When I got home at dinnertime I had some bread and dripping. Grandma used to say, "Do me a couple of slices while you're at it young lady," so I did some and then went back to school. In the afternoon we did sewing and drawing and I loved this. The boys went off to woodwork and metalwork. At teatime I had my jobs to do and no matter how quickly I worked I never had time to go out to play.

The following year when I was nine was the start of the second world war. Us kids thought it was something exciting, but also I felt very afraid of the unknown. Mother was still doing her two jobs and somehow she had changed. She always wore the same weary expression on her face and she didn't seem to have much time for me. Gone were the days when she used to tell me stories and she looked so old before her time. Harold Sutton came out into their yard next to ours and used to tell me stories about what would happen in the war. He frightened me by saying a man called Hitler would come and drop bombs on my head and when I started to cry he laughed at me. We soon found out what war was all about as we stuck sticking plaster across our windows and put black out curtains up. Nearly every home had an air raid shelter and when ours arrived we had to ask Mr Sutton to help us dig out the dirt to set it up. Some of the local men came to help and we had a box to step on to get inside. Mother put some old boxes in for us to sit on, but I didn't like it in there. We were all issued with gas masks, which we had to carry everywhere with us. At school we had to wear them for ten minutes practice every day. The school shelters were built in the playground and it was awful going in them, they were very low down and had little seats all round the sides for us to sit on. I think the worst part was the air raid sirens, when they started to wail you knew then that the air raids were about to start. At first we just had practice but one night whilst we were fast asleep in bed the siren sounded. Mr Sutton shouted to mother, "Go in the shelter Maria, I think there will be trouble tonight." I was awake by then and mother told me to get dressed quickly and she woke Grandma . Into the shelter we went but Grandma said she was staying in bed. "Good," I thought, "I hope Hitler bombs her." I told my mother when we got in the shelter and she was very cross with me although I noticed a wry smile flicker across her face.

We sat on the boxes and waited. Mrs Nelson, the policeman's wife, who lived next door on the opposite side to the Suttons, came and asked if she could come in our shelter. They hadn't been issued with one because they had no children. We sat there shivering although it wasn't cold. Mother had rigged up an old door to put over the door space so it was very dark. Suddenly we heard the sound of planes going over, their droning noise drummed in our ears. "Put your ear plugs in," said mother, so we sat in silence but we could still hear the planes. We heard a scuffle outside and the door opened. It was Grandma wrapped in a blanket wanting to join us. We struggled to get her down the step and as we did we heard the first bombs explode. I thought my ears would burst and Grandma screamed as she almost fell. Mrs Nelson held her up while mother pulled the door back in position. The bombing went on for about an hour and I was shaking with fear. Then we heard the planes going back and they sounded so different now they had dropped their bombs. Just at the top of our road was an army camp and we had already seen the big guns but had never heard them in action. On this night they opened fire on the enemy planes and the searchlights shone in the sky. Mr Sutton came to see if we were alright. He said Mrs Sutton had sent him, Harold followed after him and just as they arrived at our shelter the guns began to fire. I have never heard anything like it and Mrs Nelson put her arms round my head to cut out the sound. Grandma just sat and cried and said she needed the toilet. Mr Sutton and Harold ran back to their shelter and mother closed the door. Then we heard a friendly voice it was old John Allen who was in the Home Guard. "Don't be afraid," he said to mother, "worst is over now them buggers are going back to Germany, but the City centres taken a buffeting." "We're alright John," said mother, "just a bit shaken that's all." Ten minutes later the All Clear sounded and we trundled back to our beds. As we did so we could see the City in the distance all ablaze. Next day at school everyone was talking about the air raid and we found out from our teacher that the bombers were aiming at the steel works but had missed their target and hit the City instead. A lot of damage had been done and many people had lost their lives. This was only the start and as the years went on we slowly got used to our sleepless nights. Food was on ration and we hardly had any sweets, but mother still managed to put food on the table and hold down her two exhausting jobs. She seemed to live in a little world of her own and no matter how many times I tried to talk to her she just seemed oblivious to my existence. There was so much I wanted to tell her. School was my world and I loved every minute I was there, but whenever I tried to tell her what I had been doing she just mumbled to herself something like, Oh! don't bother me now Annie. Yes! my mother had changed so much since my father died. Memories of my dad lingered with me and I so very much wished he was still here. I wanted to tell him about my work at school, I knew he would be interested. He was quite a clever man and from the stories my Grandma Clayton used to tell me he was doing very well at school until he had to leave at eleven years old to go down the pit. Quite a different story to when I was eleven. All our class had to take the eleven plus examination. If you passed, the girls went to High School and the boys to Grammar School. Jed Harper had passed to go to the Grammar School, but his mother couldn't afford to let him go, she knew he had to go to work when he was fourteen to help her with money. So he stayed on at our Council school and left when he was fourteen to work down the pit. By now the conditions below ground were a little better but, still the life as a miner was very tough. My eleventh birthday came around and nothing had changed at home. Grandma Pointer was still sitting in her rocking chair reading her books and eating her chocolate. She was looking more wizened and miserable than ever and her life was so mundane. Mother was still working at her two jobs and was so terribly distant. I tried so hard to cheer her up but nothing I did meant anything to her.

The morning came for me to take the first of the two exams we had to take for the eleven plus. The first one was at our school and all the children in our class took the exam. We all sat at desks on our own in the big hall. The teachers gave out the papers and we were given the signal to start. We had two hours to complete the paper. I felt very apprehensive but read everything through carefully, like our teacher had told us to do, and then to write. I found it quite easy and after one and half hours I had completed the task. When the two hours were up the bell rang and we all had to stop. The teachers collected up our papers and we were able to go home. Mum was at work as usual and Grandma greeted me with her usual grunt. "I've taken an exam today Grandma," I said, "I shall go to the High School if I pass." "I don't know why you are wasting your time," she replied, "your mother can't afford to send you to High School so stop having bright ideas beyond your means, and get the kettle on and make me a cup of tea." I felt so down as I lifted the heavy kettle and placed it on the fire. "Besides there's no call for girls to pass exams and go to posh schools," said my Grandma, "so the sooner you leave school and get a proper job in a shop or cleaning for the likes of Mrs White, the better. You know your mother needs the money, never mind exams." So I made her a cup of tea in the hope she would shut up and went about my work. I'd just got to the top of the stairs when she called, "not enough sugar in me tea, get yourself down here and do your job properly young lady." I went back down and put more sugar in her tea and as I passed it to her she hit me across the head. This time though I fell over and the mug of tea fell out of my hand. It spilt all over Grandma's lap and she yelled out, "You stupid girl, now look what you've done," and rose from her chair. Her clothes were wet through and as she got up she lashed out at me with her hand. I went flying and hit my head on the corner of the fireguard. She stood over me and rained blows at my body. I screamed for her to stop but she was like someone gone mad. Over and over again she hit me as I struggled to get to my feet. I managed to get up. "Get out of my way," she screamed, " or I will kill you." I managed to reach the bottom of the stairs and pulled the door behind me. I could feel something warm trickling down the side of my face and I put my hand up and felt. My hand was covered in blood. I was shaking with fear and didn't know what to do. Just then I heard mother's voice. "Where's our Annie?" she said to Grandma, "and what have you spilt down your front?" "She's upstairs making beds," she said, "I've only spilt me tea." Then mother heard me crying. She came to the bottom of the stairs and saw me covered in blood. "Good heavens!" she declared, "what's happened to you our Annie?" "Looks like she's fallen down stairs," said Grandma, "I thought I heard a bump." Mother helped me into the room. "Did you fall lass?" she said, and I knew from the look on Grandma's face that I had better not tell the truth. "Yes mum, I did," I said. "Come here," she said, " let's get some water and wash all this blood away." Mother held me over the sink and cleaned my head but as fast as she did it still kept bleeding. "I'm going to fetch Ivy Parsons," she said to Grandma, "look after her while I'm gone." Mother dashed out of the door and Grandma came over to where I was sitting next to the sink. She grabbed hold of my arm and pushed me off the chair and gave me another whack. "Don't you dare tell anyone it was me that did it or I'll kill you," she said, and gave me another punch. Mother came back with Ivy Parsons. "Oh! my God, you must have gone a pearler," she said, "let me look luv," and she held my head and wiped the blood away with the cloth mother had used. "I think she will need some stitches in that," she remarked. "But I can't afford to take her to the doctors," said mother. "I think you need to send for him," she replied. "I'll send our Ned up to surgery and get him to come." "I can't let the doctor come here," said mother, "it will cost twice as much." I could feel the hot sticky fluid running down my face and I was frightened. The more Ivy Parsons tried to stop it the worse it bled. "Hold this towel to her head and I'll go and get doctor." Off she went and mother sat with me. Grandma just moaned about her wet dress and stood in front of the fire trying to get it dry.

Ivy Parsons came back and said she's sent their Ned. An hour later we saw the doctor coming up our path. I'd never seen our doctor before but he looked very nice and kind. "Now young lady," he said, "lets have a look at you." He examined my head and cleaned the wound. "I'm going to have to put a few stitches in there," he said to my mother. "Now this might hurt a bit," he said to me, "but try and be brave." Mother held my hand and Ivy Parsons leaned over to look. I felt a sharp pain and I let out a yell. "Try not to cry," said my mother, so I gritted my teeth till he had finished. My head was throbbing and I felt that I wanted to cry but I was too weak.

"Now how did this happen?" said Dr Parkin. "She fell down stairs," said mother. "But this wound isn't consistent with a fall downstairs," said the doctor as he was writing out a prescription for some tablets for me to take. "I'll ask you once more Annie, how did this happen?" I started to cry and huge sobs shook my body. I must have looked at Grandma because mother let go of my hand and went over to her. "It's you isn't it?" she said, "you've been hitting her again, haven't you?" "Oh! I only tapped her," said Grandma, "it's time she was taken in hand."

The doctor finished his writing and went over to my Grandma, "You haven't heard the last of this," he said, "now keep her quiet for a few days and then bring her to see me at the surgery and I will remove the stitches, you will get my bill when the treatment is over," and with that he went. Mother took me up to bed and I laid down with my head pounding. "I'll bring you up some broth," she said and went down stairs. Then I heard their voices. Mother was screaming at Grandma and Grandma was answering back. Then everything went quiet as I fell asleep. After this incident my Grandma never laid a hand on me again. I made a good recovery and was soon back at school.

Chapter 10

I had been off school for two days and mother was at home all the time, this I couldn't understand. I wondered if she was staying at home to keep an eye on me, or had something happened at work. When I went back to school all my friends were pleased to see me, and my teacher, Miss Firth, made a real fuss of me. I was excused games and P.E. and I soon caught up with the work I had missed. It seemed funny having my mum at home when I got in, but she just looked more worried than ever. I decided I would ask her why she hadn't gone to work. "Mum, what are you doing at home all the time," I said. "I've lost my job at the wash house," she said, "it closed down at the weekend so I've got to find something else to do, I'm going after a job today though down at Johnson's." "What will you be doing there?" I said. "Oh! they are wanting cleaners," she replied. "I hope you get it Mum, but I do wish you could do something better." "I've not had any training love to do any other kind of work and we do need the money," she replied. The following week she started cleaning at Johnson's, she started at six in the morning till two in the afternoon. Johnson's was a big factory making cutlery, but because of the war, had to change over to making weapons. It was a dirty job and mother came home filthy, then she had to go to scrub floors at the hospital, but she earned better money than at the wash house so our lives were a little easier. We still spent time in the shelters most nights the sirens sounded and our sleep was disturbed. Yet the war seemed to bring people closer together and although life was tough somehow we managed to keep going.

One morning at school our teacher announced that the results of the exams we had taken had come through and Mr Wright, our headmaster would announce them in assembly. Apparently fifteen children had passed and would be going on to the next exam. As we all filed into the hall I felt very excited. Mary Ashton and me stood together and after we had said prayers and sung two hymns, Mr Wright stood up and began talking. My heart was bursting inside me and when he said he had got the list in front of him with the names of the children who had passed, I thought my heart would burst. "I will read the names in alphabetical order," he said, "first, Jean Burton." I looked at Mary and she was near to tears, next Annie Clayton," and so he went on. I'd heard my name and couldn't believe it. I just didn't hear any of the other names but when I looked at poor Mary I just longed to put my arms around her. I nearly didn't hear when Mr Wright called us all to the front of the school hall, and as I walked up with the other children my heart was beating fast. When I got home at lunch time, I didn't bother to tell Grandma. I just did the bread and dripping, ate it and went back to school. At tea time I told my mother. She gave me a hug and said, "Well done, but don't get too excited, you may not do so well next time." Then Grandma went on about what a waste of time it was for a girl to have an education. Mother told her to shut up, something she had been doing a lot lately.

After my mother finished work at the hospital that night I was allowed to stay up a bit later and mother and me walked across to see my Grandma Clayton. She hadn't been very well but when she saw us she brightened up no end. Mother gave her the two loaves she had baked and asked how she was keeping. "I'm a lot better now," she said, but I could tell from her eyes she was far from well. "Go on then," said mother, "tell her your news." I had never seen mother look so happy for a long time. I thought it was because I had passed my exam, but I soon found out differently. "I have passed my first exam to go to the High School," I said and Grandma lifted me on to her knee and gave me a big hug. "I am so pleased for you my dear," she said and I could see a tear trickle down her face. "There'll be such good opportunities for you when you get older." Two of my dad's brothers still lived at home and whilst we were there they came in from their shift down the pit. By now Grandma had a bath fitted in her house with lovely hot running water. Both Uncle Gerald and Uncle Bob were pleased to see us and after they'd asked how we all were, prepared to go into the bathroom. "Don't go just yet," said Grandma, "our Annie here has some news for you." So I proceeded to tell them about passing my exam. Uncle Gerald picked me up in his big grubby arms and danced around the floor with me. "I knew we had some brains in the family," he said, and as he put me down Uncle Bob gave me a sixpence. I felt so happy. When I went to bed that night I couldn't get to sleep for excitement and when I said my prayers I prayed I would pass the next exam.

One night my mother came home from work and said she was going out. "You will go to bed like a good girl," said mother. I was now old enough to get myself ready for bed. "Make yourself some cocoa," she said, "and there are some biscuits in the tin." It's not very often we had biscuits and I wondered what had come over my mum. "Where are you going?" said Grandma. "Oh! just going out with some friends," said mother. "You've no right to be going out," said Grandma, "what if the sirens sound?" "Don't worry," said mother, " if the sirens sound I will come straight home," and she started getting ready to go out. I had never seen my mum looking so pretty for a long time. It looked as if she'd bought herself a new blouse and it was the first time I'd seen her wearing make up. She gave me last minute instructions and gave me a kiss and off she went.

I had some homework to do, so I settled down at the table and started my work. Grandma looked up from her book and said, "What are you up to young lady?" "I'm doing my homework," I said. "Well make me a cup of tea and pass me them biscuits," she said. So I dutifully did as she asked. When I wasn't looking she pried into my work. "This looks rubbish to me," she said and leaned over and knocked my bottle of ink all over the place. "Oh Grandma look what you've done," I said, and tried to retrieve my books, there was ink everywhere. Grandma sat back down in her chair whilst I tried to mop everything up. "That wasn't fair," I said, with tears in my eyes, but Grandma just munched on her biscuit and ignored my distress. After I cleaned up the mess I decided to make my cocoa and go to bed, I'd got a book I could read in bed and I knew she couldn't get at me up there. So I made my drink and went to get a biscuit, the empty packet was on the table she had eaten them all. I climbed into bed and picked up my book, 'The Three Musketeers' by Alexander Dumas. I had only read three pages when the siren sounded. 'Gosh they're early tonight,' I thought and put on my cardigan and went downstairs. Grandma was asleep in her rocking chair. "Grandma the sirens are going," I said with alarm. "Oh! go back to bed," she said, "we'll be alright." So I went back to my bed, I could hear the bombers coming over so I put my head under the bedclothes and tried not to listen. Suddenly there was a terrific explosion followed by another and another, our house fair shook. I jumped out of bed and ran downstairs. Grandma was sitting upright in her chair. "Quick," she said, "into the shelter." Grabbing my coat I ran outside. The air was thick with dust. I reached the shelter in record time with Grandma following after me. "Are you alright," said a voice, it was Mr Sutton who had just shepherded his wife and son into their shelter. "Where's Maria?" he said. "Gone gallivanting off out," replied my Grandma. Just then I heard mother's voice, she climbed into the shelter but she wasn't on her own. Following closely behind was a young man, he climbed in after mother just after another wave of bombs were dropped. "My God," said Grandma, "we are all going to die and who are you young man?" "This is Alfie Burrows mother, we have been for a walk." Grandma grunted and mother sat next to me and enquired if I was all right. We were in the shelter for nearly four hours and when the all clear sounded we stumbled back in doors. Our house was still standing but all the windows had been blown out and soot was everywhere. Some of our neighbour's houses had been flattened and there was dust and soot still hanging in the air. We learnt that Johnson's factory had taken a direct hit so mother was out of work once more. When things had settled down we learnt that two people had lost their lives and quite a few had been injured so we had been lucky.

Chapter II

After that night we saw quite a bit of Alfie Burrows, I quite liked this softly spoken man who was making my mother so happy. Although he didn't have the good looks of my dad, he was quite presentable with his fair hair and nice face. He was much taller than my dad had been and seemed to tower over my mother, but it was nice having him around and I found out my mother had met him at work. He soon got another job driving buses and eventually my mother became a conductress and worked along side him. She was able to give up her hospital job and although she worked odd hours she was much happier. Grandma grumbled every time she saw him but mother managed to ignore her. I didn't have so many jobs to do when I arrived home from school, so I was able to go out and play with my friends. What a difference this made to my life, I usually met up with the Harper boys and Jed always paid me a lot of attention. I felt so sorry for him because I knew the burden of helping look after his mother and his brothers fell on his shoulders.

Then the day of the second exam was announced and we had to go to the High School to take this exam. Out of the fifteen who had passed six of us were girls. Entering the High School was so nerve racking I thought I would have forgotten all I had learnt. We had to sit in the big hall with all the other girls and everyone looked scared stiff. I sat in my place and looked around. Round the hall were pictures of old members of the school and everything was very regal. Then we received our papers, the bell went for us to start, and I felt sick with apprehension. I read through the papers and it might have been written in double dutch. A feeling of panic swept over me as the invigilators walked past our desks, but after a while I calmed down and began to write. Somehow I managed to get through all the questions and put my pen down with a sigh of relief as the final bell went. On the bus home I talked to the others about what we had written and I felt convinced I had failed. When I arrived home mother was already up, she was working on the night shift this week. She put my tea on the table and asked me how I'd gone on. "Oh! mum I'm sure I've failed," I said. "Don't be silly love you'll be alright," she replied. "I told you it was a waste of time," said Grandma, "there's nowt in it for girls." "Oh! mother keep quiet," said mum, "can't you see Annie is upset." "Needs a good hiding to my way of thinking," said Grandma. Mother ignored her and I proceeded to tell her about the exam. Next day at school Mr Wright sent for me and the other five girls who had taken the exam. We gently knocked on his door and soon we were sitting round his desk. "Well girls, how did it go?" asked Mr Wright with a happy smile on his face, "You first Annie Clayton." I felt my face go bright red and I started to talk but my voice wouldn't work. "Well sir," I said eventually, " I don't think I've done very well." "Why is that?" he said. "I found the questions very difficult but I did the best I could," I replied. "Well that is good," he answered, "I think you will find you will be alright." The same question was put to all the others and we nearly all gave the same reply. When we had all said our piece he sat in his big swivel chair and talked to us for about half an hour. What he said made such sense and we all came out of his room feeling much calmer.

When I reached home I told mother about going in to see Mr Wright and she was so pleased he had talked to us. "Now go out and play and forget all about this exam till you get the results." So off out I went to the local quarry where all our gang were playing kick can. I soon joined in and completely forgot about the beastly exam. Two weeks later Miss Firth announced, whilst we were having register, that the results had come through and once again Mr Wright would tell us at assembly the names of the people who had passed. We all filed into the hall and had our usual prayers and hymns. I was beginning to feel sick with apprehension. Mr Wright stood in front of the whole school and made his announcement, "I have received this morning the results of the eleven plus examinations taken by the following children." He proceeded to read out the names of all the boys and girls who had taken the exam. "I will start with the names of the boys who have passed, and I will read them in alphabetical order." So his voice went on, only three of the boys had passed out of the nine who took part. "Will you boys come and stand at the front with me," he said. The three boys with their happy faces went and stood with Mr Wright. I looked round at the other boys who had failed and they looked so sad. 'That will be me,' I thought in a few minutes time. "Now for the girls," he said, "only one girl has failed so here we go with the successful five. "First is Annie Clayton," he said and then he carried on with the other names. I felt so happy I couldn't move and when he called us to the front I couldn't believe I'd done it. All the children clapped us and for the rest of the day I was in a whirl. I felt sorry for Jean Burton and she couldn't stop crying. Miss Firth sent for her mother to take her home. I rushed home to tell my mother, and we danced around the room together. Grandma sat grumbling because her tea wasn't ready and mother said we will go over and see grandma Clayton tonight to tell her the news.

Alfie Burrows arrived at six o'clock and we all set off across the village to see Grandma Clayton. When I saw her face I couldn't believe how ill she looked but she still gave me a big hug and sat me on her knee. "Now young lady, what have you come for?" she said. "Wait a minute," said my mother, "let me introduce you to my friend Alfie Burrows, we have been going out together for some time now, and Alfie has asked me to marry him, I wanted you to be the first to know." Mother looked so very happy and Grandma got up out of her chair and gave my mum a hug and shook hands with Alfie. "I'm so pleased for you both," said Grandma, "I give you my blessing and all the happiness you deserve." Then she turned to me, "and what about you young lady?" she said. "I was so happy to hear mum's news I nearly forgot what I had come for. "Go on then, tell her," said mother. "I have passed the second exam for the High School Grandma," I said. "Oh! this is good news," she said and put her arms around me and held me close. "You are just like a tonic to me you are," she said, "I am so happy for you all." All that was left for me to do now was to get through the final exam. But I had no need to worry, when the day came all we had to do was go and talk to the headmistress at the High School and just answer the questions she put to us. When I knew I'd been accepted I was over the moon.

Chapter 12

During the summer holidays, my mum and Alfie Burrows were married in a very quiet ceremony, which only Uncle Gerald and me attended. Grandma Clayton wasn't well enough and Grandma Pointer refused to go. The night before the wedding my mum sat on my bed and talked to me, "I shall never stop loving your dad," she said, "he was my first love but Alfie has made me very happy and I want you to know you will always be first in my heart." I climbed out of bed and put my arms round mother. We didn't speak, but we both knew our memories of Jim Clayton, my lovely father would never die. It seemed strange having a man about the house again, Alfie Burrows fitted in so well and used to sing along in our new bathroom. Yes, we now had a new bath and hot running water. The old scullery had been changed and we had a lovely new bath and washbowl in there. Every day before he went to work you could hear him singing all the latest songs. Grandma used to grumble about the noise but I liked to hear him. It seemed so much safer having him around when the air raid siren sounded, he helped us all into the shelter. "I think it's time we took you to get your school uniform," said my mum one day. "But where will you get the money from," I said, " and what about clothing coupons?" "Oh! don't worry about that," said my mum. So off we went to Mantons, the big haberdashery shop in town. We had a list of clothing I needed and I was so excited. I tried on various items, two dark green gymslips and a dark green blazer with a gold badge on the top pocket, a panama hat and two cream boat necked blouses. I had two pairs of all the underwear I needed. Long black stockings and lovely black patent shoes, and when mother came to pay the bill I was so worried. "Mum, where did you get this sort of money from?" I said. "Never you mind," she replied, "just don't worry about it, I want you to do well at school, and that will be all the payment I will need." It wasn't until I was in my late teens that I found out, Grandma Clayton, Uncle Gerald and Uncle Bob had helped my mother out with the money and coupons. On the way home we got off the bus where my Grandma Clayton lived. "Why are we getting off here mum?" I asked. "We're going to see your Grandma and show her your uniform," she answered. So I skipped up the street where she lived. It always seemed dirtier round here because her house was nearer the pit than ours. Grandma was sitting in the corner and the room was dark. As we went in mum went over to where Grandma was sitting. "Are you alright?" she said. Grandma seemed to be asleep. This was a strange thing for her, she was usually in the kitchen bustling about. "Oh! hello our Maria, it's you," she said, opening her eyes. "I was falling asleep, I'll put the kettle on." "No you won't," said my mum, "you sit still and I'll make us a cup of tea." "Hello young lady," she said to me, "you seem to grow more every time I see you." "Hello Grandma," I said and put my arms round her frail old body and gave her a kiss. "I've come to show you my school uniform," I said. "Oh! that is nice of you, I need cheering up a bit." So mother started opening the bags. "Cost us a fortune she did," said Alfie and gave Grandma a wink. "These things look lovely," said Grandma," go in the front room and try them on for me."

Mother followed me into the front room and I put on my new clothes once more. "Are you ready Grandma?" I called, "close your eyes I am coming." I walked back into the living room and Grandma was sitting with her eyes closed tight. "You can open them now," said Alfie. Grandma opened her eyes and looked at me. "My you look a right picture," she said, "how like your dad you are getting, come here and let me look closer, he would have been so proud of you if he'd been here," and tears rolled down her face as she held me close. "Come on now, no more tears," said my mum and we all drank our tea.

As we were walking home from Grandmas, the sirens started wailing. "We had better hurry," said Archie, so we ran most of the way home. We got to our house just in time to hear the German planes coming over. Grandma Pointer was standing at the door. "Where have you been till now?" she said, "you don't care about me." "Into the shelter quick," said Archie, ignoring Grandma's wailing. It was unusual for a raid to start whilst it was daylight. As I looked up I could see the German planes high in the sky. Our guns started to roar and I was shaking with fright. Suddenly we heard a terrific bang and a shout from the gunners at the anti-aircraft gun site. "We've got one," they yelled and we heard the whirring of the doomed plane as it hurtled to the ground. The loaded plane hit the ground in old farmer Barber's field.The heavy bombs exploded and we were all deafened. Alfie calmed us down and poked his head out of the shelter. All we could hear was the fire engine bells as they raced to the burning plane. "Stay where you are," yelled the men on home guard duty. So we sat trembling in the shelter till the all clear sounded. When we returned to our house we learned that most of the steel works had taken direct hits and were left in ruins. When I went to bed and saw my lovely school uniform hung on the dresser the excitement of the day seemed irrelevant.

Chapter 13

I started my new school in September 1941 and after the initial beginners fears, I soon settled in. I made some lovely new friends and, although the work was difficult I loved every minute. Every night I had loads of homework but never grumbled.

One day I was going out to catch the school bus I noticed mother in the bathroom and she was very sick. "What's wrong mum?" I said. "Oh! I'm alright sweetheart," she replied, "but I've got something to tell you." "What is it mum?" I said, feeling very worried. "I'm going to have a baby," she said, "and sometimes when you are having a baby it makes you feel sick." "Oh! mum, I am so pleased, but will you be alright?" "Of course I will, I'm still young and I am very happy." I went to school and couldn't wait to tell my friends. Mother gave up her job and it was lovely to have her at home all the time. The only thing that made me unhappy was my lovely Grandma Clayton was so very ill and she was always in and out of hospital. Grandma Pointer still sat in her corner rocking away with her books and her chocolate, she seemed to get more grumpier as she got older, but I had learnt to ignore her. Then one day just before my twelfth birthday we were told Grandma Clayton had died. Uncle Gerald came to let us know. Her poor kind heart had at last stopped beating, she was only seventy. After the funeral everyone came back to our house and I couldn't believe I would never see her again.

I came home from school one day and saw Nurse Barker's bike leaning up outside our house. I knew it was near to mum having the baby and I felt very nervous as I went in. Alfie was drinking tea and looking very worried. I could hear a commotion upstairs. "How is my mum?" I asked. "Baby's on its way," said Alfie, "it won't be long now before you have a little brother or sister." I was so excited. "Why don't you go out and play with your friends," he said, "and I will call you when it's all over." "But can't I stay here and help?" I replied. "There's now't you can do," said Grandma Pointer, "so get off out with you." So I changed my clothes and went to call for Mary. We decided to go and find the other kids and soon we were playing rounders. Jed Harper was there with his brothers and I felt so sorry for him because when he finished school this year he was going to work in the pit.

After I had been out playing for a couple of hours Mary's mother called her in for her tea. I followed her to our house and Nurse Barker was still there. As I went through the door I could hear a baby screaming. "I was just coming to find you," said Alfie, "you have a little brother." "Oh! how lovely," I yelled and put my arms around Alfie. He had tears in his eyes. "Can I see him?" I said. "In just a few minutes," replied Alfie. Nurse Barker came downstairs and told me I could go up and see my mum and my little brother. Alfie followed me upstairs and there was my mum with my baby brother in her arms. I walked across and looked at him and he opened his lovely big blue eyes as if to say 'Hello' to me. He was beautiful. Although my mum looked very tired, she also looked very happy. "What do you think to your little brother?" my mum whispered. "Oh! he's lovely mum, how soon before I can hold him?" I said. "Come and sit at the side of me on the bed," said mum. So I climbed on the comfy eiderdown at the side of my mum and she put the baby in my arms. I held him tight and he wrinkled his little nose and snuggled up close to me. He was lovely. "What are we going to call him?" I said. "What about you choosing a name," said Alfie. I thought for a minute and said, "What about Edward?" Mum looked at Alfie and said, "That's a name I like, what about you Alfie?" "Yes that sounds nice, Edward Burrows, that'll do for me lass, but I would like to give him a second name." "Oh! what would that be?" said mother. "I'd like his middle name to be James, if that's alright with you," he said. "What a lovely thought," replied mum and we all agreed Edward James Burrows it would be.

Chapter 14

Yes, Edward James Burrows soon settled into our family life and when I came home from school I couldn't wait to take him out in his pram. He was a lovely baby and very content. Mother looked so happy and our lives seemed to have more meaning and when the war drew to an end in 1945 everyone rejoiced that this terrible time was over. My schoolwork seemed generally good and when my parents attended the school to discuss with my tutor what I wanted to do when I had finished school, all I could talk about was becoming a teacher. I wanted to teach English and I never had my nose out of a book. Then the time came for me to go to University, I had never been away from home before, and I felt very nervous but also very keen to start my teacher training. I would miss all my friends, especially Mary, who was now working as a hairdressing apprentice. Also I would miss Jed Harper, he was a special friend, and when he wasn't working we would often go for walks together. We would talk about all our hopes for the future and he would tell me what it was like down the pit and how he hoped one day to be able to give up the terrible job and do something different. He still looked after his mother and also his brother Jacky was working down the pit with him with Billy joining them next year.

Just before I started at University my mum received notification that she had to get out of the house we lived in, because Alfie did not work at the pit she was told they could not live in a pit house. My mother was very distressed and pleaded with the pit manager to let them stay, but he was new to the job since old Mr White had died, and wouldn't listen to my mother. So mum went to see Tom Bratley, who was now retired. "I'll see what I can do for thee lass," he said, "but I don't hold out much hope." Mum thanked him and came back home with a heavy heart. The following week she was sent for to face the manager of the housing department. "Sit down Mrs Burrows," he said, "I'll get straight to the point," and with his miserable face he turned to my mum. "What right do you think you have to live in a pit house?" he said. My mum turned on him in such a fury. "My husband Jim Clayton was killed in the pit, just for your information," she said. "But that was years ago," replied the officious man, "now you are married to someone who has no connection with the pit." "I suppose losing my husband doesn't stand for anything now, does it?" replied my mum, "anyway where can I go, you just can't put me out on the streets." "You must apply to the council," he replied. No end of pleading from my mother made any difference.

On her way home she called at the council housing office and told them of her plight. The man listened carefully to her, but didn't offer much hope. When she arrived home she was very distressed and there was nothing either Alfie or me could do to cheer her up. Little Edward slept through all the upset and when he woke, even his beaming smile did nothing to make my mum any happier. "What's wrong with you our Maria?" said my Grandma. "Nothing that concerns you," replied my mum. "Well you could have fooled me," said Grandma. "I shall be glad when I am dead," she carried on. "Grandma you don't mean that," I said, "my mum needs cheering up not to hear you talking about dying." "Who do you think you're talking to young lady?" she said, "you've got too big for your boots since you've gone to that High school." "Stop it now you two," said Alfie, "surely you can see how upset she is!" and put his arms round my mum. "Don't worry too much love, I am sure we will sort something out." So we ate our teas and tried to forget the problem we had ahead of us.

Two days later my mum received a letter from the pit office saying that her request to stay in this house had been granted, we were so relieved.

Chapter 15

Just before my sixteenth birthday I was studying for my school certificate. I worked very hard and I didn't get out very often. When I did go out I usually met up with my friends from my old school, most of them were working and they seemed more mature than me. We usually went for a walk and on Saturday evening went to the dance, which was held in the school hall. I loved to dance and mum and Archie used to come and bring little Edward. In fact all families enjoyed the Saturday night outing. All the families with young children went home early but I was allowed to stay till the end at ten o'clock. Most of the time I danced with Jed Harper and when Harold Sutton came to dance with me, I got really cross. Jed always walked me home and he put his arm around me. The first time he kissed me, I was so happy.

When my exams began I worked so hard. I wanted to repay my mum for everything she had done for me and when July came round I found I had passed all the eight subjects I had taken. My best results were in English language and English literature. I was so pleased how things had gone and I was so determined to carry on and work hard for my entrance exams for university. I was seeing Jed Harper quite regularly now and everybody thought of us as boy and girl friend. He came to our house and we spent endless hours playing with little Edward, which gave my mum and Archie chance to go out together occasionally.

I soon settled back at school after the summer holidays and continued to see Jed. He was working shifts down the pit so it wasn't very often we had the chance to be together. Mum had talked to me about being careful when I was with Jed, but we were so very much in love. One night we were walking in the local woods when suddenly he held me in his arms and asked me to marry him. "We are too young," I replied, "and I want to finish my education, but I do love you Jed with all my heart." That evening we made love. I was so naive and didn't realise just what was happening. Jed was so careful and gentle, I cried in his arms. "I will always love you," he said, as we lay together in the long grass. I had given myself so freely and it felt so right that we now belonged to each other. We walked home with our arms entwined and I felt very grown up. As we kissed 'Goodnight' no words were needed.

Just before Christmas, as I sat in Dr. Smith's surgery, my fears were confirmed, I was pregnant. Dr. Smith had examined me and asked a lot of questions and suggested that I now go home and talk things through with my mother. Mother was sitting in the waiting room, and as we walked away from the surgery I dare not look her in the face. "I think we will walk home," she said. I expect this will give her time to tell me off, I thought to myself, but as we walked along she tucked my arm in hers. It was a while before she spoke, and, as we crossed the common, she turned to me and said, "You have made a big mistake my Annie, but I will help you all I can." I watched the tears roll down her cheeks and I tucked my arm tighter into hers. What a brave and understanding mother I had, there were no recriminations, no shouting and telling off just an offer of help. I felt so humble after I had let her down so badly. "What am I going to do?" I said at last. "We shall have to go round and see Jed Harper and find out if he is prepared to marry you," she said. "Oh! mum, do I have to get married?" I replied. "Of course you do, you can't bring a baby into this world without being married," she replied. "But what about school?" I answered. "We shall have to go and see Miss Rhodes and tell her you will be leaving." The thought of having to leave school and the enormity of getting married and becoming a mother filled me with the most dreadful fear, but not to be able to finish my education was about the worst thing that could happen.

"What about Alfie and Grandma?" I said. "Leave them to me," said mother, "I will sort them out." When we arrived home Alfie was at home looking after Edward and Grandma demanded her lunch. I went straight upstairs and lay on my bed and sobbed till I thought my heart would break. When mother called me for my lunch I went downstairs, and as I went into the living room little Edward ran towards me and put his little hands in mine. Alfie put his arms around me and held me close and told me not to worry as he would look after me. This brought fresh tears till mother said, "Come on you two your dinner's getting cold." Grandma just looked at me and gave a grunt and got on with her dinner.

That night, after Edward was put to bed we walked round to Jed Harper's house. His mother invited us in and looked very concerned. "What is the trouble?" she asked, "come and sit down and I will put the kettle on." I looked around this spotless house and wondered how she was able to manage so well with so many children to look after. She came back from the scullery and gave me and my mum a nice hot cup of tea. "You look worried stiff Maria, can I help at all," she said, and sat down across from us. "It's our Annie," replied mother, "she's having your Jed's baby."

Betty Harper's face changed immediately. "Oh no!" she exclaimed, "I am so sorry." She came over to where I was sitting. "My poor love," she said as she put her arm around my shoulders. "What are we going to do?" Our Jed will be home from work in an hour, will you stop until he gets here." "No, we will get off and if you don't mind, will you tell him for us?" said mother. Up to now I hadn't spoken, "I want to tell him myself," I said. "I'm sorry love but I think this business is out of your hands now," said mother, and with that we got up and set off for home. Mrs Harper saw us out of the door and I felt like a small child without any backbone at all.

We hadn't been home very long when there was a knock at our door. Standing there with his cap in his hands was my Jed. He looked so upset I just wanted to hug him. Mother invited him in. "Hello Jed," she said, "I'm so glad you have called round." "I'm so sorry Mrs Burrows," replied Jed, "will you please forgive me, but I love Annie so very much and I will always look after her." I went over to where he was standing and he turned to me. "Forgive me Annie I'm so sorry," he said. "There is nothing to forgive Jed," I replied, "I love you too." Grandma looked up from her book and said, "Look what you've done to our Annie, you want horse whipping young man." "Less of that talk mother," my mum replied, "this is no business of yours, so keep your mouth shut." Grandma was about to reply, but thought better of it.

"The best thing we can do now is to get things sorted out," said my mum. "Of course I will do the right thing and we will be married," said Jed. "I was hoping you would say that," replied mother, "I was just going to say we must get the wedding arranged." The thought had not come into my head that we would get married, I could not think of myself as a married woman. Grandma piped in, "You'd better get rid of that babby," she said, "old Iris Shackleton in't next street would soon get rid." "Mother, I won't tell you again, keep out of it, our Annie will be married and they can live with us till they get a place of their own," said mother, her temper rising.

If I thought this family get together had been upsetting the worst was yet to come. My mum and me had an appointment to see our head teacher, Miss Rhodes. Mum put on her best coat and off we went. We were ushered into Miss Rhode's office, a place I had only been in once before. I looked around at the shelves of books and the big oak desk in the middle of the room. Miss Rhodes sat in her swivel chair and beckoned us to sit opposite her. We took our seats and my legs were trembling. "Now, Mrs Burrows what seems to be the trouble and why hasn't Annie been attending school?" she asked. Mother cleared her throat and began to speak. "Well it's like this," she said, "Annie is pregnant." Miss Rhodes looked very alarmed. "Oh, my goodness I am so sorry," she said, "this is a dreadful shame, she has so much potential." She came over to where I was sitting. I turned my head in shame. "Look at me child," she said in her school marm voice, "you are not the first this has happened to and you won't be the last, I am just so sorry it happened just now when you had such a lot going for you." Not one word of chastisement. "Well there is nothing for it but for you to leave school, I will get on with the arrangements and good luck to you and your baby when it arrives." She shook mother's hand and we were on our way home in no time. I felt so humiliated and went home and lay on my bed and cried into my pillow

Chapter 16

The wedding arrangements were made and Jed moved his things across to our house. Mum and Archie bought us a double bed and a wardrobe, and the day of the wedding dawned. I had a new frock to wear and we all caught the bus to the Registry Office. Jed was waiting for me wearing a new suit and his brother and mother were sitting behind him. He had asked Steven Bratley to be his best man and when I stood beside him and we took our vows I knew I loved him with all my heart. After the ceremony we caught the bus to our house and we had sandwiches and cake, and when everyone had gone home that night I realised I was not Annie Clayton anymore but Annie Harper and I felt such pride. All my doubts about leaving school had vanished and I declared I would make Jed a good wife. We shared our double bed and Jed was such a gentle lover and gradually our lives settled in to a routine. I felt so well during my pregnancy and began to look forward to our baby arriving.

Two days after my seventeenth birthday on the 14th June I knew things had started. I called to my mum as Jed was at work. She sent for Nurse Barker and when she examined me she said, "Yes you are in labour but there's a long way to go yet, so put on your nightie and get into bed, I've got someone else to see to but I'll be back shortly," and off she cycled. It was nearly two hours later when she came back, by now I was in such excruciating pain and Nurse Barker examined me and said, "Looks like it won't be long now, I'd better get scrubbed up." Mother came in with a pan of boiling water and held my hand as I started to push, I was screaming in agony and mum mopped my brow with a cold cloth. Nurse Barker told me to push and I could feel my baby arriving into the world. "Keep pushing dear," she said, "your baby's head is here, right just one more push, that's right now no more pushing, you've got a lovely little girl." I laid back and breathed a sigh of relief. "Is she alright," said my mum as we heard the cry of my baby. "She's just fine," said Nurse Barker, "she's got some right lungs on her, let me just clean you up and get your baby weighed and then you can hold her." Mum propped me up with pillows and Nurse Barker handed me my baby. "She weighs seven and a half pounds," she said, and as I took her into my arms I couldn't believe how beautiful she was. She had a mop of dark hair just like her dad and she was gorgeous. Nurse Barker cleaned me up, while mum held the baby, and said she would have to be on her way but would call back later. "Put her to your breast," she said, but I felt so weak and tired I wasn't listening. After Nurse Barker had gone mum put the baby in the make shift cot, this consisted of a drawer lined with blankets. She said to me, "Try and have a little rest and I will bring you some broth." I laid back on my pillow and mother went downstairs. Suddenly there was a knock on the bedroom door. "Can I come and see you?" and Alfie popped his head round the door. I was too tired to answer and he bent and looked at my baby and he beamed with pride. "Oh! she is lovely Annie, you've done a good job there," he said. He carefully touched the baby's face and turned to me and said, "Good luck to you Annie love, you know your mum and me will always be here for you."

I could feel myself dozing off to sleep when Nurse Barker returned. She checked the baby and cleaned me up. I felt much fresher and when she left she said she would be back next morning. "Keep putting her to your breast," she said and with that she was gone. The only sound I wanted to hear was my Jed coming home from work and I watched the clock as time drew near for him to arrive. I picked up my baby and held her close. I couldn't believe that she was mine. Mum came up later and brought me my tea and little Edward was with her. He was a lovely little boy and he leaned over and looked at my baby and was so very careful. "Can I hold her?" he said, and I gently lifted her out of her cot and told him to climb on to the bed at the side of me and I put her in his arms. The memories of this happening to me came back from when I held my baby brother Edward in my arms. When I heard Jed's voice I was so excited. He leapt up the stairs and burst into the bedroom. "Oh! my darling, are you alright," he said, and held me in his arms and we cried together. "Let me have a look at her," he said. He pulled back the blanket and she opened her eyes and looked up. "You are beautiful," he said, "can I hold her?" "Of course you can," I answered, and he carefully lifted her out of her cot and held her close in his arms. "My darling you are wonderful," he said to me, "do you feel alright?" "Yes, I am alright," I answered, "but I am very tired." "What are we going to call her," he said. "I don't know, you choose a name," I replied. "What about Alison," he said. "That is lovely," I said, "Alison Harper, that sounds very nice."

The time passed quickly and soon my two weeks stay in bed was over and I was able to get up once more. Nurse Barker had visited me every day and Alison was feeding well. I came down stairs for the first time and Grandma Pointer greeted me with, "Let's have a look at her then, she's made enough cat-a-wailing while you've been up there." I took Alison across to her and she looked at her, "Not the prettiest one I've seen," she said, "you've been a fool Annie Clayton getting pregnant at your age, but you never were very bright to start off with," and turned back to her book. If mum had been there she would have had something to say to her but she had gone to the shops and I felt too weak to argue.

So we settled into a lovely routine and Alison thrived in the summer sun. When she was three months old we were informed that we had been allocated a pit house. It was at the other side of the village from where we lived, quite near to my Grandma Clayton's house. Uncle Gerald lived there now and he was married. All the boys were now married and had homes of their own. We went to look at our house when Jed got home from work. There was no bathing in front of the fire now as all the miners had baths at the pithead. We walked across the village pushing Alison in the pram and Mum, Archie and little Edward following behind. We all looked for number 99 Colliery Terrace, I had the key safely in my coat pocket, and when we arrived at the house I couldn't wait to go in. It was a bit like my Grandma Clayton's house, two rooms downstairs and a small bathroom and two bedrooms upstairs. There was a cooking range with a big black oven at the side of the fire and a big sink under the window. The toilet was down the yard but the house was clean and I knew we could make it cosy. Mum said she would do the papering and Betty Harper gave us a settee and a table and two chairs, so armed with our few possessions we moved into our freshly decorated house.

It was lovely to be on our own and not to listen to my Grandma's grumbling. I'd always tried to keep Alison quiet when she was near, but I couldn't always manage it and so she grumbled. I had a little fear as my periods had not returned after Alison's birth and I put it down to the fact that I was breast feeding, but somehow I didn't feel right. I decided to go and see Dr. Smith and he examined me when I told him how I felt. "You are four months pregnant, at least," he said. I felt myself keel over and he took Alison out of my arms. When I came round he gave me a drink of water. "Come on now," he said, "it could be worse." How I got home that day I do not know. When Jed came in from work there was no tea on the table and I just sat and cried. "What's wrong?" said Jed, his face full of worry. He put his arms around me and held me close. "I'm pregnant," I said between my sobs. "Oh! no," said Jed, "this can't be true." "But it is," I answered, "I've been to see Dr. Smith today and he says I'm four months gone." "Don't worry love I will look after you," he said, "and to think we shall have a nice little brother or sister for Alison." "But we can hardly afford to live as we are," I answered. "I will do more overtime at work," he said, "now let's not worry any more." The next day I went round to see my mum. "Hello! love," she said, "it's lovely to see you, come and sit down and I'll put the kettle on." She lifted Alison out of her pram and sat her on the floor. Edward came across to play with her and they looked so happy playing together. Grandma didn't even lift her eyes up from her book. Mum passed me my tea and sat down beside me. "How are you love?" she said, "you don't look very happy, is everything alright between you and Jed?" "Yes mum we are alright," I answered, "but I've got something to tell you, you see I've found out I'm pregnant again and the baby is due on Alison's birthday."

"God help you my love," she said, "but try not to worry everything happens for a reason." So as Alison's first birthday approached I tried not to let things get me down and prepared myself for my second child's birth.

Chapter 17

This baby came much easier and my mum and Nurse Barker were with me once again. Another little girl weighing eight pounds two ounces was placed into my arms exactly one day after Alison's first birthday. I couldn't believe I was now only eighteen and I had two little girls. Jed was just as thrilled and helped me as much as he could and when I was up and about again little Joanne was an untold joy. If I thought Alison was a good baby, this one was twice as good. She slept right through the night and I hardly knew she was here, and as she grew they were such good company together. The only down side was poor old Jed, he was having to work such long hours to keep us. My mum helped me as much as she could, but now Edward was at school she had got herself a part time job at the local corner shop. My Grandma was still sitting in her old rocking chair reading her books and now she was older she was even more cantankerous. All she ever seemed to do was pray to die and her attitude really got my mother down.

Joanne was only three months old when I realised I was pregnant again. I was so upset and went round to see my mother. When I told her I fully expected her to be really cross. I sat and cried and mother put her arm around me. "It doesn't matter love," she said, "what is meant to be, will be." "But mother what am I going to do," I said, "we have all on managing as it is but with another mouth to feed it will be a real struggle." She held me in her arms as I sobbed. "What's up wi you two," Grandma butted in. "Nothing to do with you mother," said mum. "Bet she's pregnant again isn't she?" she added, "silly young fool having all them kids." "Just ignore her," said mum as the sobs shook my body. So time went by and our third daughter was born just after Joanne's first birthday. She was a lovely baby and weighed nine pounds. We christened her Sally and gradually our lives settled down once more. Our little girls were a real handful, but I enjoyed every minute I spent with them. I often wondered what my life would have been like if I had carried on with my education, but I was so happy with my Jed and my lovely little family that I put any thoughts of being a teacher to the back of my mind. I was frightened I might become pregnant again but Jed and I were so much in love, I put my fears on hold and tried to get on with my life. But, when Sally was just at the toddling stage, I realised my fourth baby was on it's way. Baby number four, Angela arrived safely and she was just as gorgeous as the other three. My mum spent so much time at our house, I don't know what I would have done without her. Nurse Barker seemed to be always at our house, but she never gave me any lectures about having so many babies, and when Natalie arrived the following year I was just about exhausted. I was only twenty two and my life just seemed to be one round of nappies and feeding but the children were good and we had lots of fun.

One night I had just got up to settle little Natalie off to sleep, she was a colicky baby and I looked at the clock, it was two thirty. I had just got back into bed, Jed was on the night shift, when I heard the pit hooter wailing. This was a red alert warning so I knew something was wrong. I went downstairs and put the light on. I knew there was nothing I could do. I made a cup of tea and sat on the kitchen stool. I held my head in my hands and waited. Suddenly there was a knock at the door, it was my mum. "I thought I'd find you up," she said. "What's happened mum?" I said. "I don't know love," she replied, "but put your coat on and get off to the pit."

I went out into the cold night air and made my way in the gloom to the pithead. I met Doris Porter down the street, we didn't speak but made our way to the pithead and stood with the other women. "What's happened?" said Maureen Hoskins to one of the deputies. "Sorry love," he said, "I don't know what's really happened, but there's been a fall of earth down there and we think some of the men are trapped. My heart stopped beating as I clung on to Doris Porter's arm. "Oh! my God, what will become of them," she said. The rescue workers were already down there and all we could do was wait. My memories went back to when I was there with my mother and my Grandmas and I couldn't stop shaking. Working in the pit was supposed to be so much safer now and I couldn't believe this was happening.

We stood there in the shivering cold and everything was quiet. In fact the eerie silence that prevailed caused a sense of foreboding. No one was about until suddenly the pit cage clanged to the top. It was so dark we couldn't see if anyone was in the cage. We heard voices and the panic stricken faces appeared in the gloom. "Clear the way," yelled one man, and the injured men were stretchered out of the cage. In the distance I could hear the sound of the ambulances arriving and I looked up to the sky and saw the first signs of snow falling. I ran with the other women to where the stretchered men lay, but we were not allowed near. All we could hear was the moaning and groaning of our poor men folk.

I must find out what happened to my Jed I thought to myself. I went up to one of the rescuers and shouted to him, "Have you found Jed Harper?" "I don't know love, all I know there's still some men down there and these poor buggers are in a right mess." "What happened?" I continued. "Heavy fall of muck love, roof weren't shored up properly," he said. I tried to peer through the darkness but couldn't see any of the men's faces. "Better go home love," said a kindly voice, "not much you can do here." I turned and saw the face of Steven Bratley, old Tom's son. "I must know what's happened to my Jed," I replied. "Can't help you, you must go home and someone will come and let you know what has happened," he said. I wended my weary way back up our street. Mum was sitting in the kitchen holding my baby in her arms. The other girls were fast asleep. "What's happened love?" she asked. "I don't know mum," I said as I knocked the snow off my shoes, "there's a lot of men injured, there's been a bad fall, and us women were getting in the way." "Come and sit down and hold on to your bairn and I'll put the kettle on." So I took little Natalie into my arms and looked at her beautiful face, so like her dads, and sat and sobbed my heart out. Mum passed me a cup of tea and slowly my tension was released as my little girls began to wake and came and sat with me.

Chapter 18

The doctors and nurses were waiting at the hospital as the injured men began to arrive. Quickly and efficiently they were dealt with. Sister Doherty was just about to go home from the night shift when she heard about the pit tragedy. Although she was tired, she decided to stay and see if she could help. She was so near to retirement and couldn't wait to return to her native Ireland. She quickly walked along the corridor to where the men were being treated. "What can I do?" she asked Dr Brownlow. "Just help settle the men in their beds," he said, "most of them have gone to surgery." So off she went to the private rooms where the victims were being attended. One by one she made them comfortable until she came to one bed and lying there was a familiar face, although covered in grime this face stood out. Her memory went back to the lovely man she had sat with many years ago. She looked closer and the unconscious man seemed so familiar. A name came into her head, "Jed Harper," she exclaimed. She looked at the name at the bottom of the bed and sure enough, Jed Harper stood out. This was too much to take in. She pulled a chair up to the side of the bed and sat down and reached for his hand. She felt faint and as she looked at this handsome man, her memories returned to that dreadful night so many years ago. She hummed softly and then said a little prayer and moved on to the next bed. When all the men were settled comfortably she walked back and took one more look at the unconscious Jed Harper. Under her breath she said, "Good bye, dear friend, please be still here when I come back tonight," and with that she collected her belongings and went home to her bed. Morning dawned and Annie was busy getting her little girls ready for school. No one had been to see her so she decided when she had taken the children to school she would call round at the pit. She wrapped the children up warm and was just about to set off when Steven Bratley appeared at the door. "Oh! I'm glad I've caught you," he said. "Any news," I asked. I couldn't stop shaking. "Yes," he said, "your Jed was one of the first out, but I'm afraid he's badly injured." "Oh! my God," I said as I steadied myself on the pram handle. "What is wrong?" "He took the brunt of the fall," he said, "and has suffered very bad head injuries," he continued. "I must go to him, what will I do?" Mum was at work and I didn't know who would look after my babies. The only person I could think of was Grandma Pointer and she was now so old I didn't know whether I dare take the risk of leaving them with her, but I was so desperate.

I walked into the house and sure enough she was still sitting in her rocking chair. Her sight was now so bad she didn't realise it was me. "Hello Grandma," I said. "Oh! it's you is it, what do you want?" "I wondered if you could help me?" I said. "Why what's up?" she replied. I quickly explained my circumstances and she turned and peered at me over her glasses. "If you think I'm looking after them bloody kids, you've got another think coming," she said, "shouldn't have had so many in't first place, serves you right if he deas," and with that she went back to her book. I stood and looked round the old familiar room where I had spent my childhood. The memories were not happy ones and I wrapped my children up warm and turned and left the house. "Can't we stay at Grandma's," said little Sally, "my feet are cold." "No sweetheart," I answered, " we are going home." "But my legs are tired," she protested. So I sat her on the pram with Angela and Natalie. I pushed them along, the snow getting thicker and I felt so full of despair I knew I would have to wait till my mum came round this afternoon before I could go to see my Jed. I fetched Alison and Joanne from school and by four o'clock I was on the bus to the hospital.

I asked at the reception where Jed Harper was and was informed he was not allowed visitors. When I explained who I was, I was asked to wait in reception. Sitting there my thoughts turned to Jed's dad and the way he died and I felt sick with apprehension. Suddenly I looked up and standing before me was a man in a white coat with a stethoscope round his neck. "Hello, Mrs Harper," he said, "I'm James Brownlow the doctor in charge of your husband." I looked at his tired face and tears rolled down my cheeks. "If you'd like to come this way," he said, "I will try and explain what is happening to your husband." He didn't speak again until we arrived at his room. "Please sit down," he said, and beckoned me to a chair. He stood with his back to me, "Well, Mrs Harper what I have got to tell you isn't very good news, I'm afraid your husband has received very serious head injuries and the next few days are crucial, even if he did pull through, I just don't know what his future holds." "What do you mean?" I cried, "Do you mean he will be permanently damaged?" "We don't really know," he said, "but time can be a great healer," and then proceeded to explain the nature of his injuries. I didn't really understand much of what he was talking about and all I wanted was to go and see him. "You can have half an hour with him," he said, and led me along the corridor to where he was. As I approached his room I could hear a faint voice singing, "Oh Danny boy the pipes the pipes are calling," the lovely lilting voice reached me from my husband's bedside. I walked into the room and sitting there at the side of my Jed was a lovely old nurse holding his hand. He looked so peaceful lying there and apart from the heavy bandages round his head he looked as if he was fast asleep. As I walked through the door she turned her head and let go of Jed's hand. "Oh, I am sorry," she said, as she got up from her chair, "I didn't mean to intrude." "That's alright," I replied, "please don't go." She turned and looked at me, "You'll be Mrs Harper," she said, in her soft lilting voice, "Please let me introduce myself, I'm Sister Doherty, Mary Doherty that is." She went on, "I was just trying to comfort your poor husband," and she came towards me and put her arms around me and I sobbed on her shoulder. "There, my dear, don't be so upset," she said, "I am sure the Lord above is watching over you." She led me to the bed and said, "I will leave you two alone, try to be brave," and with that she gently let go of me and left me alone with my Jed.

I leaned over and looked at his tired face and touched his cheek gently with my fingers. "Hello, my darling," I whispered, "I am here with you now," and I pulled up the chair and took his hand in mine and gazed at his face. He didn't move at all whilst I was with him and I didn't know what to do. The doctor had told me he had had major surgery and there were tubes coming from his body and a heart monitor bleeped in the corner. A nurse came into the room and checked him over. "What can I do?" I said to her. "Just be with him, that's all he needs at the moment," she said, and left the room.

My grief was so overwhelming and when I was told to leave the room and go home, I felt numb with pain. How I got home that night I will never know. Mother was waiting for me, she had just finished putting my girls to bed. When she saw my face, she knew things were bad. "Come and sit down love you look all in," she said. "Oh mother I don't know what to do," I said, as I fell into the chair. "Why, what's wrong, how is he?" she said. I proceeded to tell her about the terrible mess he was in and I felt sick with apprehension. I couldn't stop shaking and mother made me a cup of hot strong tea. "Try not to worry too much," she said, "your Jed is young and strong and I am sure he will be alright." "But mum you haven't seen him, I think he is going to die," I replied. "Now let's have less of that talk," she answered, "do you want me to stay here tonight?" "No, I'll be alright," I answered, "you get off home." Just then I heard a noise on the stairs, I got up out of my chair and opened the stair's door. There sitting on the bottom step were my two eldest daughters, Alison and Joanne. "What are you doing out of bed?" I asked. Alison looked up, "Sorry mum," she said, "but we were worried about you," and Joanne started to cry. "Come here the two of you," I said, and led them into the room. They both sat on my knee and I held them close. "Where is dad?" said Joanne, "when will he be home?" "It's alright mum," I said, "leave it to me, you get your coat on and get off back to your Alfie, I'll be alright." So off she went into the cold night air. I held my girls tight and tried to explain, as best I could, what had happened to their dad. Eventually they were falling asleep on my lap so I gently took them back to their beds. The two of them slept together and the three younger ones slept in one big bed so it did not disturb them as I settled them down. I tidied up the kitchen and decided to go to bed myself, but sleep evaded me. I could see Jed's face so calm and still and I couldn't help but worry that he would not pull through. What would become of us, I could not live my life without him.

Chapter 19

Next day I tried to keep things as normal as possible. I took my eldest two girls to school and came back home and left the other three to play while I tried to get on with the washing and ironing. I couldn't wait for my mum to get here at four o'clock so I could go off to the hospital. I imagined that because I hadn't heard any news about Jed, he must be all right, so I caught the bus to go and see him and did my best to feel more optimistic. As I travelled along the familiar route I tried to ignore the now familiar feeling that I was pregnant again. I was only twenty four and I had five little girls, but I knew deep down that another baby was on its way. I walked into the hospital and went straight to my husband's room. I gently opened the door and Mary Doherty was sitting there singing softly to my Jed. As I walked in she got up to leave, "Oh! please don't go," I said, "please stay and talk to me, how is he today?" and I looked at his face and knew there was little change. "I think he seems better," she declared. "Please don't lie to me," I said, and sat down and looked at his dear familiar face. "I'm so sorry," said Mary Doherty, "I just wanted to cheer you up, you look so lost, yes, you are right there is no change in his condition, but I would love to tell you he is improving." Tears welled in her bright blue eyes and we sat together and said a little prayer. I began to talk about my education and how I had hopes of becoming a teacher and how Jed and me had fallen in love and our five little girls were born. I then told her about my fears of being pregnant again and how worried I was about the future. "Your children were sent for a purpose," she said, "and they were born out of your love for one another." "I am sure the dear Lord above will look after you and you must look forward and count your blessings." I knew this was true and somehow I felt better for talking to Mary Doherty. After a little while she got up and left and I sat there stroking my husband's cheek as if to will him to come round. I started to talk to him and told him about my fears of being pregnant again but there was no reaction. I just wanted him to reassure me that everything would be all right. Dr Brownlow came into the room, "Hello Mrs Harper," he said, "how are you today?" "Alright doctor," I replied, "but what is going to become of my husband?" "It's early days yet," he answered, "Mr Harper has very severe head injuries, and is the most severely injured of all the miners. I am afraid I am going to be blunt with you my dear. There isn't much hope of him making a full recovery. He has a blood clot on his brain and even if he does recover, he will be severely disabled. I am so sorry to have to give you this sad news," he continued, "but all we can now do is to take good care of him and pray for a miracle to happen." I felt myself go faint and clung on to the bed covers for support. The doctor came round and stood beside me whilst a young nurse appeared with a glass of water. "Here drink this," he said, and held the water to my lips. The room was spinning round and I keeled over. As I came round someone was holding my head, through my blurred vision I could see Mary Doherty. She held me close and talked very gently to me. "Come on my dear, let me take you home," she said. I picked up my bags and got to my feet. My legs felt like jelly as I walked along the corridor. Mary Doherty held on to me and outside was a waiting taxi. Mary sat beside me and soon we were whisked back to my home. Mary helped me in. My mum was feeding Natalie and the other girls were in their nighties ready for bed. "My goodness Annie," said mother, "what on earth has happened, you look terrible." Mary Doherty took over as she took off my coat and sat me in the chair. My girls gathered round me and I felt sick with worry. "Make her a good strong cup of tea and a little brandy in it, if you have any," said Mary, and she introduced herself to my mother. I sipped the hot sweet tea but I couldn't stop shaking. Mum had searched for some brandy but I knew we hadn't any. I tried to focus my attention on my children, but they looked so bewildered.

Mary took mother into the front room and explained what had happened at the hospital. Mother decided there and then she would stay all night with me. Mary gave mum a tablet for me to take when I went to bed and when she left us I was beginning to come round a little. Between us we settled the girls off to bed after trying to answer their endless questions and mother and me sat and talked well into the night. As I lay in our big double bed, I could not sleep. I was so distraught even the tablet I had taken had no effect at all. My thoughts were with my poor Jed and I prayed as I had never prayed before. When daylight dawned I felt a little figure creeping into bed beside me. It was my little Alison. She was now eight years old and mature beyond her years. She snuggled down beside me and whispered in my ear, "I love you Mummy and I will look after you." With those words I fell into a fitful sleep. The next thing I knew my mother was at my bedside. On a tray there was tea and toast. "Come on sleeping beauty," she said with a forced lilt in her voice. I looked at the bedside clock, it was ten o'clock. "Mother whatever is happening," I said. "Don't worry love everything is alright, I have taken the children to school and the two little ones are eating their porridge." "But what about your job?" I asked with alarm in my voice. "That's alright, I called in to see Mr Meadows, and he said I had no need to go in today. Now eat up your toast and you will feel much better," and off she went down stairs to see to Angela and Natalie. I tried to nibble on my toast but I felt sick so I drank my tea and lay back on my pillows. After a while I heard voices downstairs. I reached for my dressing gown and went to see who it was. Standing in the kitchen was Mary Doherty. "Oh! my God what's happened," I said. "It's alright Annie, I've just called round to tell you there is a slight improvement in Jed's condition," she said, so I thought I would come and let you know, it's not much but Dr Brownlow checked him over and he seems to think his breathing is better." I went over to her and gave her a hug. "Just let me get dressed and I will come back with you to the hospital." "Will you be alright mum?" I asked. "Of course I will," she replied. I quickly dressed and washed and we were soon on the bus back to the hospital. I looked at the little Irish lady with such a lovely face and I couldn't thank her enough for her care.

We rushed along the corridor and into Jed's room. Nothing had changed, he was still lying in the same position but his colour seemed better and his breathing certainly seemed easier. Mary stood behind me. "Go on speak to him," she said. I bent closer to him and said, "Come on big guy, it's time you woke up." There was no response so I sat down at the side of his bed and held his hand. "I will go now," said Mary. "No, please stay," I said, "I want you here with me." So she pulled up a chair at the other side of the bed and held Jed's other hand. She started humming in her soft lilting voice something about the hills of Killarney and I found her voice so very soothing. At least an hour must have passed and not a word was spoken between us. The duty nurse popped her head round the door. "Bet you two would like a cup of tea?" she said and disappeared down the corridor. Ten minutes later she was back and the lovely steaming hot tea was much appreciated. We were then asked to leave the room while the nurses saw to my Jed. When we got back his dressings had been changed and he had had a bed bath and clean bedding. He looked much better. "Dr Frazer is on his way to see Mr Harper," said one nurse to Mary. "Who is Dr Frazer?" I asked. "He's only the finest brain surgeon in these parts," said Mary, "look I think I'll run along now if you are alright and let Dr Frazer talk to you on your own." "Ok, Mary and thanks for all you've done," I replied.

I sat there in anticipation and sure enough ten minutes later a small, bright ginger haired Scotsman came into the room. "Good morning to you my wee lassie," he said as he came over and shook my hand. "You'll be Mrs Harper?" "Yes, that's right," I replied. "Now let me see, your husband was in the Bristow mine was he not? Well my dear I have looked at his x-rays and I'm afraid the news isn't good, as I suppose you know, but I am going to have another look at him to see if there is anything more we can do," he continued, "I don't hold out much hope but if you would like to go home now and come back again tomorrow afternoon it will give me chance to re-assess his condition." I thanked him profusely and made my way back home. When I got in mother had made a big pan of broth. I didn't realise I was hungry, but when I sat at the table and she placed this lovely bowl of broth in front of me, I fairly wolfed it down. I started to speak, but mother soon shut me up and told me to get on with my food. I felt like a little girl again and I was so grateful she was looking after me.

When I had finished eating she rattled on about what she had been doing and how well the children had behaved. Out on the line was all my washing and the children were clean and happy. I then got chance to tell her about Dr Frazer. Mother was just as pleased as me but warned me not to raise my hopes too high. Then she surprised me when she said, "When is the baby due then?" "Oh! mother," I said, "how do you know?" "Never mind how I know, I just know that's all." "But I haven't told anyone except Mary Doherty," I said. "Yes! but I only have to look at you to know," she replied. I was so surprised I didn't know what to say. When I had recovered my composure I said, "I'm about three months gone." "Well good luck love," she replied, "here's hoping this one's a little lad, it will give your Jed something to live for."

I walked to school and fetched my three eldest girls and that night mother went home. The hours dragged by and I didn't sleep a wink. Somehow I managed to get the children off to school and came back and got on with my chores. At eleven o'clock I heard a knock at the door, I had just settled Natalie off in her cot to have a little sleep and Angela was busy at the table colouring a picture. I went to the door and Mary Doherty was standing there. She looked flustered. "Hello Mary," I said, "what brings you here?" "I'm sorry Annie," she said, as she bustled into the kitchen, "but I'm afraid it's bad news, your Jed has taken a turn for the worse." "I'm so sorry," and tears welled in her eyes, "I got here as quickly as I could," she said. I felt my legs turn to jelly and I had all on keeping my balance.

"Mary what can I do?" I heard my voice quaking. "Go and get the next bus to the hospital," she said, "I will stay and look after your babies." "But Mary you've been on the night shift, you must be tired," I replied. "Never mind me," her voice lilted on, "go and get the next bus as quick as you can." I looked at the clock and realised the next bus was twenty past eleven. I grabbed my coat and purse and set off for the bus stop. As I was approaching I could see the bus coming in the distance. I started to run but the bus driver didn't see me and he was gone before I got there. I stood there trying to catch my breath and I was feeling sick and dizzy. I didn't know what to do and I leaned against the lamp post for support. I knew the next bus was in another twenty minutes and I so wanted to be with my Jed. I looked up at the sky as the rain clouds gathered and I prayed to God to help me. I shivered in my well-worn coat as the rain began to pour when suddenly a passing car slowed down and stopped. The driver wound down the window. "I thought it was you Annie Clayton," said the driver. Who can this be, I didn't know anyone with a car, and why was he calling me Annie Clayton, I thought to myself. The old man looked familiar and then I realised it was old Mr Sutton who used to live next to us when I was little. "Oh! hello Mr Sutton," I said. "Where are you going to?" he asked, "can I give you a lift." "Please if you will, I have just missed the bus and it's twenty minutes till the next one," I replied as I climbed into the passenger seat. "I am going to the hospital to see my Jed," I said, as tears rolled down my cheeks. "What is wrong with him Annie?" he replied. "Didn't you know he was badly hurt in the pit accident?" I said. "No, I didn't," he replied, "I know about the accident but didn't know about Jed, I am so sorry. If there is anything I can do please don't hesitate to ask. Are you sure you will be alright?" "I'll be alright Mr Sutton, and thanks for the lift," I said, and off he drove.

I walked into the hospital and made my way to Jed's ward. Sister stopped me and said, "Hello Mrs Harper, please come with me, Dr Brownlow would like to speak to you." She took me to his room and there was no one there. "Would you care to sit down, Dr Brownlow will be with you in a moment," she said. "But I want to see my Jed," I cried. Dr Brownlow appeared at the door and sat on the edge of his desk. He cleared his throat and started to speak, "I'm so sorry Mrs Harper but your husband passed away about half an hour ago, there was nothing more we could do for him and he never regained consciousness." The room closed in on me as I felt myself slump off the chair. When I came round the doctor was bending over me. He held a drink to my mouth and I felt the liquid trickle down my throat. "Take me to my Jed," I cried. "Later," said the doctor, "we must deal with you first." "But I'm alright," I said, as I tried to get up I felt my legs buckle under me. "I must go to him," I ranted on, "please take me to him." My demented cries echoed round the room. "I have sent for your mother," said Dr Brownlow, "and as soon as she arrives I will take you to your husband." It seemed an eternity till my mum arrived and she came to me and held my head in her arms and we clung together. After a while we left the room. I clung onto my mother's arm with Dr Brownlow leading the way. We approached a large old building and Dr Brownlow quickly unlocked the door. In we went and he led us into a small side room. The room was dark till he pulled back the blind. Lying on a slab in the middle of the room was my Jed. Dr Brownlow quickly left us and I moved over to where Jed was laying. He looked as if he was fast asleep. Mother sat near the window. I put my arm out and reached for him. "Come back to me my darling," I whispered, "please don't leave me." I held him in my arms and pressed my face close to his and cried till I thought my heart would break. Mother didn't disturb me and I held on to his lifeless body till my arms ached. Slowly my strength began to ebb and I sat back on the chair and stared at his handsome face and I knew my dear husband had gone and I was now on my own to face this dreadful life without my one and only love. My Jed.

Chapter 20

My children gathered round me as we prepared to follow the hearse. Slowly the cars wended their way to the church and we walked behind the coffin as it was laid to rest on the funeral bier. The service began and I looked at my little girls and put my hand on my protruding belly and I knew from that moment on my life would be dedicated to my lovely children. I had no tears left and as they lowered my husband's coffin into the grave as near to my dad's as I could get it, I knew I would spend my life looking after the lovely children we had produced with our undying love.

The next few days went by and I felt numb with grief. Automatically I fed my girls and the two eldest were so much comfort to me, they were like little mothers fussing round the little ones and doing all they could to ease my pain. I don't know what was going on in their minds because now they were old enough to understand that their beloved father would never be here for them. People called to see us and my dear mother eased most of my hurt. She had problems of her own, my Grandma Pointer wasn't well and was causing my mum a lot of trouble, and my mother in law, Betty was a tower of strength although her grief was very deep having lost her eldest son. Old Mrs Sutton came round one afternoon and sat and talked to me. She was a lovely old lady and she reminisced about the old days. I walked part way home with her and the children and I realised this was the first time I had been out since the funeral. It was good to feel the sun on my face and as I walked along with my daughters running around me I felt fresh hope for the future.

One night as I was sitting having five minutes after all my girls were in bed, I started to take stock of my life. I was now twenty-eight years old and about to become a mother again soon. I had no money and life looked very bleak. I sat with my head in my hands, I had no more tears left to shed when my eldest daughter crept downstairs. "Hello sweetheart," I said, " are you alright?" "I couldn't get to sleep mum," she replied, "so I thought I would come and keep you company." She pulled up a stool at the side of me and we sat and talked. I was surprised at the knowledge she had and we talked about her plans for the future. "When I leave school," she said, "I will get a job and help you." "But what about going to High School and having a career?" I answered. "Oh! it doesn't matter about my education," she replied, "I would rather earn some money and help you." "But next year you take your eleven plus examinations," I said, "what if you pass to go to High school you must go if you can," and I knew she was quite capable of passing her exams. Both my eldest girls were doing well at school, I always had good reports about their academic progress. Sally was still in the infant's school and she was mad about animals. Angela and Natalie were still at home with me and were soon to be joined by a little brother or sister. I turned to Alison, "would you like a nice cup of cocoa," I said, "and we can talk another day about your education." So I made us both a nice warm drink and soon she went back to bed.

Two days later Steven Bratley called to see me. "Hello Steven," I said, "do come in and sit down." He took off his cap and sat on the chair just inside the back door. "Hope you don't mind my calling to see you," he said, "only I was wondering how you are getting on." "I'm not too bad Steven," I said, "I don't think I've realised what's happened yet, I think it will dawn on me after a while, you see I have my girls to keep me busy and the time just flies by, the nights are the longest but I am coping." "Oh! that's good," he replied, "but I wanted to ask you if you are going to apply for compensation?" "I don't know if I'm entitled to any," I said. "Of course you are, and if you will let me help you I will show you how to go about getting it," he replied. I knew Steven had a good job with a firm of accountants in town so I knew if anyone could help me he could. "That is very kind of you," I said. "Right leave it with me and I will pick up the relevant forms for you to fill in." With that he put his cap back on and left. "Who was that man mummy?" said little Natalie. "He's an old friend of mine from my school days," I replied, "he's going to try and get some money for us to live on." Angela looked up from her picture that she was drawing and said, "That's a good thing mummy, isn't it?" I couldn't help but smile to myself.

The next day I decided that after the girls had gone to school I would go out. I hadn't seen Mary Doherty since the funeral so I thought I would make an effort and go round to the hospital to see if she was alright. After I had left the girls in the school playground I caught the bus to the hospital. I walked up to the reception desk and the memories came flooding back. The receptionist asked if she could help me. I felt quite faint and wondered if I had done the right thing in coming back so soon. "Are you alright," said the young girl as I held on to the desk for support. "Yes I'm fine," I said, "I am looking for Sister Mary Doherty." "Please sit down and wait a moment and I will try and locate her. Will you give me your name and I will let her know you are here."

I trundled the pushchair and my two little girls and sat in the nearest chair. It was good to sit down. A few minutes passed and the girl came back and beckoned me over. "I have been in contact with Sister Mary Doherty," she said, "she has been ill and is on sick leave at the moment, but if you would like to go and see her she is in Block 4, Flat 2 of the nurses quarters. She told me which way to go and I walked across the quadrangle to where she lived. "Where are we going mummy?" said Angela, "my legs are tired and I want a drink." I plonked her on the pushchair at the side of Natalie and hurried across the square. I quickly found Mary's flat and rang the bell. She opened the door and invited us in. She put her arms around me and we stood in a great big hug. "Oh! Mary what has been wrong with you?" I asked, as I looked at her tired face. "I've had a dose of flu," she said, "but I am so much better now." "But why didn't you let me know?" I replied. "Don't you think you've got enough on your plate without me bothering you," she answered, "but do come and sit down and let me put the kettle on, you look all in." She came back from the kitchen with milk and biscuits for the children and quickly made us a cup of tea. "How are you my dear?" she said, "it must be getting near your time." "Yes! I've only three weeks to go," I answered, and we drank our hot sweet tea. "How will you manage?" she asked. "Oh! I'll be alright my mum is coming round when the baby is born and she will stay a couple of days, it's all been arranged." "I wish I could do more to help you," she answered, "but I will come and see you when I can." "That's good of you," I said. "How are you managing financially?" she asked. I proceeded to tell her about Steven Bratley saying he would help me to get some compensation. "I should hope to goodness you will," she said, "but if I can help out, please let me know. I've got a little put away for my retirement but I wouldn't see you without." Mary was due to retire this year and she was going back to her native Ireland. I knew I would miss her terribly.

We got up to go home and she was so grateful we had been to see her. "God take care of you," she said as we said goodbye and she slipped some coins in my children's' pockets. When we arrived home, Steven Bratley was just getting out of his car. "Hello, Annie," he said, "I'm glad I've caught you." "Come in Steven," I said, as I unlocked the door, "sit down, and I will make you a drink." I made the children a sandwich and poured us both a cup of tea. "Good news for you," said Steven, "I've made enquiries and I've set the ball rolling and you should receive a fair amount of compensation. Apparently a meeting is to be held to discuss your case and I have been asked to let you know that a Mr Fullerton will be coming to see you to tell you the outcome." "My goodness Steven this is good news, I'm so very grateful, when is he coming?" I replied. "It will be next week I believe," he said, "but they will write to you and let you know." I thanked him profusely and we sat and chatted till it was time to fetch the girls from school. He was such a nice person and I did enjoy his company.

Two days later I received a letter telling me Mr Fullerton would be calling at 10-00 the following Thursday morning, I was so excited. Sure enough at ten o'clock a dapper little man came walking up my backyard. A swift knock at the door and in came Mr Fullerton. He shook my hand and said how sorry he was that I had lost my husband. He then took papers out of his briefcase and we sat together at the kitchen table while he explained to me what was happening. I found this man to be very haughty. He totally ignored my two little girls and just wanted to get this business over and done with as quickly as possible. He cleared his throat and spoke in a squeaky voice. "Well Mrs Harper the board and I have studied your case and decided you will receive £100 lump sum and £10 per week for the rest of your life providing you do not re-marry. We also grant you the tenancy of this house providing you stay a widow and do not take in lodgers. Have you any questions?" If you can say I was in a state of shock you would be right. My first desire had been to cut this man down to size but, after he had given me such good news, I didn't know what to say. He must have noticed my confused state because he turned to me and said, "Are you happy with our decisions Mrs Harper?" "Oh! Yes," I said, "it's just that you took me by surprise." "Well your case will be reviewed each year," he said, " if you will let us know of any change in you circumstances we would be obliged." With that he shook my hand and he was gone. I sat down on the nearest chair and held my head in my hands. I couldn't believe what had happened. "Are you alright mummy," said little Angela. "Yes, my darling," I replied as I picked her up and held her close. £100 to put in the bank and £10 per week to live on, I was amazed. At least now I knew I would not have to worry too much about money. My rent money was nine shillings per week and I always put a few pennies away each week for my other bills. When my girls came home from school that afternoon I quite willingly gave them all a halfpenny each to fetch a cornet from the ice cream man.

My mum called to see me that night with my brother Edward. He was quite a man now and was doing well in his chosen profession. He had always wanted to work on the land and had gone to join an agricultural college to get expert tuition. A lot of boys were still joining their fathers underground, but Edward wanted to work outdoors. When mother came in she pulled up a chair in front of the fire. The girls always gathered round her. She was listening to their stories and I couldn't get a word in edgeways. I put the kettle on and she looked at my face. "Well, come on then, how did you go on with Mr Fullerton?" "Oh! mum you'll never guess what's happened," I said, "I've been awarded a lump sum of £100 and £10 per week for the rest of my life." She got up from her chair and came over to me, "Oh! I am so pleased for you," she said and put her arms around me. We stood together and we both knew there was still a long way to go. We drank our tea and Edward kept the girls amused. They were playing games on the kitchen table and their laughter filled the room. Mother proceeded to tell me about Grandma Pointer. She was now in hospital and not expected to live much longer, and we both knew it would be a blessing if the dear Lord would take her.

That night I slept better than I had done for a long time. I had never been one to worry, but knowing I was going to receive this compensation made life seem much easier. I got up next morning and was just about to start making the girl's porridge when I felt a sharp pain deep inside my belly. I knew this was the start of my labour pains. I had ten days to go but it looked like this one was coming early. I got the children off to school and knew I would have to ring for Nurse Harris, Nurse Barker was now retired. I put Angela and Natalie's coats on and walked down the road to the phone box. I rang Nurse Harris and she said she come round straight away. I called into the shop where my mum worked and let her know what was happening. It had been arranged she would have time off when I had the baby. She spoke to Mr Meadows and said she would follow me home. I just managed to get home when my waters broke. I was in such a mess and doubled over in pain. My mum followed me in and settled me into bed. She said she would take Angela and Natalie back to her house. Nurse Harris came up the stairs. She quickly examined me and said, "This baby won't be long, and I'll just scrub up and put the kettle on." I held onto the bedpost and tried not to scream out with the pain. Nurse Harris was only a slip of a girl and very young, but she seemed to know what she was doing. The morning passed quickly and Nurse Harris never left my side. By lunchtime I was in such agony I thought I was going to die. "Oh! nurse, how much longer will this go on?" I said. "Not much longer now," she replied, "try to brave, this baby is doing nicely." By two o'clock I was ready to push and I could feel my baby emerging from my body. "One last push," said Nurse Harris, "that's it." I could hear my baby's cries as I flopped back on the pillows. "You've got a little boy," said Nurse Harris, as she gently lifted my baby up for me to see. "A little boy," I cried, "oh! I don't believe it." She cut the baby's cord and wrapped him in a sheet and laid him across my chest. I put my hand up to touch him as he screamed and screamed. Nurse Harris took him from me and cleaned him up and weighed him, he was eight pounds four ounces. She settled me down and checked I was all right and then propped me up on pillows. She placed the baby in my arms and I cuddled him to me. If I thought my girls looked like my Jed I not reckoned with my son. He was the absolute image. He had a mop of black hair and was very handsome. I stroked his little face and I sobbed as if my heart would break. "Come on now Mrs Harper," said Nurse Harris, "you must think of the future, this little fellow will bring you great joy," and she gave me a cloth to dry my tears. "What are you going to call him?" she said, trying to take my mind off my troubles. "We always said if ever we had a son we would call him Michael," I replied. "Well that's a lovely name," she answered. She fussed about clearing up and she made me nice and comfy. My baby lay on the bed at the side of me with his mop of black hair protruding from his cover. "Right Mrs Harper," she said, "I'll be on my way, I will call round at your mother's home to let her know to come back here, I'll be back at four thirty to check you over." With that she was gone.

The minute I heard the back door close, I turned and picked up my son. I released the cover, which tightly bound him, and he stretched his little pink fingers and screwed up his little face. "Hello my little Jed," I said and snuggled him close to me, the tears rolled down my cheeks. "Oh my darling Jed you should be here with me now," I spoke out loud, "we have a little son and he is your double. Why did you have to leave me, I need you so very much." All the pent up emotion seemed to flow from me and I realised I hadn't had time to grieve for my precious Jed, my one and only love. My baby opened his eyes looked up at me and I leaned back on my pillow and thanked God for sending me such a lovely bundle of love.

I must have fallen asleep for the next thing I knew I could hear voices downstairs. I opened my eyes and my baby was laid across my chest fast asleep. I sat up and rested him at my side when my mum popped her head round the door. "Alright to come in?" she said, her face beaming. "Of course mum," I cried, "where are my girls?" "Right behind me," replied mother, and soon they were all in the room. I picked up my baby and held him for them to see. "He's beautiful," said mother and the girls just wanted to touch him. "Are you alright," said mother. "Yes," I said, "just a bit tired." "Can I hold him and what are you go to call him?" she said. "Yes, take him from me he is a bit heavy," and she sat on the edge of the bed and held him for the girls to see. He started to cry and Angela and Natalie looked quite alarmed. "Don't worry girls," I said, "all babies cry." Mother passed him back to me. "You still haven't said what his name will be," said mother. "Well we always said if we had a son we would call him Michael," I answered, "but I've already been calling him Jed." Mother came and stood beside me, "I wasn't going to say anything in case I upset you but he is the image of your Jed," she answered. Just then we heard an uproar downstairs. The girls had come home from school. They bounded up the stairs and burst into my bedroom. Sally was first and she looked at her baby brother and asked if she could buy him a puppy. The two bigger girls stood at the side of me and Alison had tears in her eyes, "Isn't he lovely mum," she said, "are you alright?" "Yes, I'm fine love," I said, "just a bit tired that's all." "I'll go and make the tea," she said, she was so grown up. Joanne put her arms around me and gave me a big hug. She was the more demonstrative of the five. "Mummy," she said, "doesn't he look like daddy."? That was all I needed, here was another Jed Harper.

Each day I felt stronger and was lucky to have a home help to come in every day. She did most of the housework, washing and ironing. Mother came round at teatime and the midwife called every day, so it wasn't long before I was up and about again. Jed was such a happy and contented baby and soon my life fell into it's old routine. When Jed was five weeks old, my Grandma Pointer passed away, neither my mother or myself shed tears for her, and as I watched her coffin lowered into the grave, I felt great relief that my mother was now free of her.

Chapter 21

I knew I had to try and find some work, but who would employ me with four young children still at home. Word must have got round the village that I needed to find a job, because one night mother mentioned that Mrs White at the big house was looking for someone to help with the cleaning. Mrs White was the pit manager's wife and could afford to employ cleaners and maids to help her with the work. "Go up and see her," said mother. "Who will employ someone with young children around?" I asked. "You can but try," she answered, "and if I can help I will do my best." So I went up to the big house the next morning. I had seen the house from a distance but had never been near it, and as I approached the black wrought iron gates I felt very apprehensive. I slowly walked up the long drive with Jed in the pram and Sally, Angela and Natalie at my side. "Where are we going?" said Sally. "To see a lady and see if mummy can get some work," I replied. "Will she have a dog?" she asked. "I don't know love, we shall find out when we get there," I replied. "What if she doesn't like us?" said my little Angela. "Oh! she will like us alright, but you must be very good whilst we are there," I answered.

I approached the door and hesitated before I reached for the knocker. I was just about to turn away when the door opened. Standing there was a young girl, not much more than fifteen years old, dressed in a black dress and white frilly apron. "Can I help you?" she said. "I am looking for work," I replied, "and I understand Mrs White needs someone to help in the house." "Come in," she answered and I lifted my baby out of the pram and went inside. "Sit down," said the girl, "I will tell Mrs White you are here." I sat on the nearest seat and looked around. We were in a massive hallway with beautiful red carpet on the floor, ahead was a sweeping staircase up to the first floor. "Mummy I don't like it here," said Angela. "Don't worry love we won't be here long," I answered, and hugged her to me. Little Natalie was leaning on my lap and my baby was fast asleep. "Where will the dog be kept?" said Sally. "I don't know if they've got a dog," I answered. As I spoke Mrs White came through one of the doors. She was an elegant lady and very well dressed with her silver hair fastened in a bun at the back of her head. "Hello my dear," she said as she came towards me, "can I help you." I started to get up but she soon told me to stay where I was. "I am looking for work," I said, "and understand you need someone here." "Yes! that's right, I do need someone fairly urgently," she answered, "but why do you need work surely your husband can provide for you?" Tears came into my eyes and I stood up and started to turn away. "I'm so sorry my dear," she said, "have I said something wrong?" "My husband was killed in the pit accident in June," I said, "and I am desperate for work." I answered whilst I tried to keep calm. I walked towards the door and she put her hand on my shoulder. "Please don't go," she said, "follow me and I will order some tea," and she walked towards one of the big oak doors. I followed dutifully behind her. We entered a lovely sitting room. The furniture was in gold brocade with heavy matching curtains. "Sit down," she said, and I did as I was told. She rang a bell and a maid appeared. "Please bring some tea and cakes and drinks for the children," she ordered, and the maid left the room, and returned with a silver tray with a silver tea set and pretty china cups. There was orange juice and biscuits for the girls and they were shown out of the French doors into the garden. Mrs White called for the gardener to keep an eye on them and she quickly poured us a cup of tea. "Have a cake, my dear," she said, and handed me a plate and small cake knife. Jed woke up and smiled at me, and Mrs White remarked on what a lovely baby he was. I prayed he wouldn't cry and I ate my cake with him laid in my lap.

"Now my dear," she said, "what I need is someone to do general household jobs. Washing paintwork, cleaning silver, cleaning drawers and cupboards, generally keeping things spick and span. I have a cleaner comes every day to do the heavy work, so there would be none of that for you to do," she continued, "so how do you feel about doing that sort of work?" "The hours would be four hours a day, five days a week the pay is two shillings per hour." My mind was working overtime, I reckoned I would be earning £2 per week. "Yes, that sounds alright," I answered, "but what about the children." "Oh! I don't mind you bringing the baby and perhaps the youngest girl, but I am afraid I can't do with them all here every day," she said, "you can put the baby in his pram while you are working and perhaps bring something to keep the little girl amused." I was so grateful she was giving me this chance I said I would see what I could work out. She shook my hand and we fetched my children in from the garden and we made for the front door. She asked me to let her know the next day what my decision was and we said goodbye. I thanked her and said I would be in touch.

We walked home and my head was in the clouds. I called in to see my mum at Mr Meadow's shop. I told her what had happened and she looked at me with alarm in her face. "Who is going to look after Sally and Angela?" she said. "I don't know mother," I said, "but I have got to think of something," and with that I went home and gave the children their lunch. "Mummy why did we go to that big house?" repeated Sally. "I am looking for a job," I answered, "and the lady there needs someone to help her." "But why?" she persisted. "Well, if I don't work we won't have enough money to live on," I explained. "So if you work can we have a dog?" she answered. "No we can't," I replied, "we have enough mouths to feed without getting a dog." "I would so love a puppy," she said and looked up at me with pleading eyes. "May be one day," I said and hugged her to me. I spent the rest of the day wondering how I could solve my problem and I thought about asking Beryl Nixon who lived next door, if she could help me out. So that night after the children were in bed I put my plan into action. Mum had called and I explained what I had planned to do. "Well," said mum, "you can but go and ask her." So I went round next door. Beryl Nixon had been my neighbour for the last five years. She was roughly the same age as me and had two young boys. Her husband worked in the pit and although she had lived there all that time, I didn't know her very well. She seemed a very nice person but was very private in her ways. I can but ask, I thought to myself. I crossed the back yard and knocked at the door. Beryl came to the door and said, "Hello Annie, do come in, what can I do for you?" I followed her in to my identical house. Her kitchen was spick and span. "Sit down," she said, and offered me a kitchen chair. "Are you alright Annie?" she asked. "Yes thank you," I replied, "and how are you?" "I'm well," she answered, "and hoping this one will be a girl." "Oh! I didn't know you were expecting," I declared. "I've only just had it confirmed myself," she replied, " and I'm so happy, but what can I do for you?" She put the kettle on and I told her about my job. "What I was wondering ," I said, "is whether you could look after Sally and Angela for me whilst I am at the big house, I would pay you something out of my wages, if it wouldn't be too much for you." She sat down and poured us both a cup of tea. "It won't be long before Sally starts school, so then there would only be Angela," I continued. She looked at me and sipped her tea. "Well I don't see why not," she said, " they could play with my Robert and John, yes I am sure I can manage it, but I must talk to Bob first before I agree." I thanked her and told her what a weight she had taken off my mind. I drank my tea and she said she would let me know before next morning came along.

The next day I was getting the children off to school when Beryl knocked at the door. Sally opened the door and invited her in. "Mum it's Auntie Beryl," she called to me upstairs. I came down and she told me she would have the girls. I was so pleased I could have given her a hug. I agreed to pay her five shillings a week and so I was able to start work at the big house. The work was laborious and boring but I soon settled into my routine and the children seemed happy with the arrangements. Beryl did a good job looking after the girls. Sally started school in September and just after Christmas Beryl gave birth to her daughter. She had only Angela of my brood to look after and seemed to be coping very well. The following September Angela started school, so there was only Natalie and Jed left at home. Jed was a good baby and was growing very quickly and although I felt very lonely I was always so busy I didn't have time to think about what my life would have been like if my lovely Jed had still been here.

The following year my eldest daughter, Alison passed her eleven plus exams and started at the girl's High School, followed the next year by her sister Joanne. I felt so very proud when I saw them off on the school bus in their identical school uniforms. Sally and Angela were now at school, so there was just Natalie and Jed at home. Jed was growing into a lovely little boy, full of fun and mischief. My life just seemed one endless round of housework, food, and school. But this was all I needed and sometimes when I felt lonely in my big double bed, I would think of my Jed and longed to be in his arms again. Life was a struggle and sometimes I would cry, but my lovely children always came to my rescue. The day that Jed started school I was talking to Miss Dakin, my old school teacher. She was now head of the school and very near to retirement. "Have you got five minutes to spare," she asked. "Yes, of course," I said, "Let me just get all the children settled, I would like to talk to you." "Would you wait in my office?" I wandered over to the office and went inside. "Make yourself comfortable, I won't be long," she said. I sat down on the nearest chair and looked around the room. I had only been in here a couple of times when I was at this school, so the place wasn't very familiar to me. I couldn't think what she wanted me for, but it wasn't long before I found out. Miss Dakin sat at the other side of the desk. She was a dear old lady and had been a very good teacher. All the children thought the world of her and she had a lovely way with them. She cleared her throat and then asked me how I was getting on. "Oh! alright," I answered. "Life must be a struggle," she said, "I often think about you and wonder how you are coping. Your children are a credit to you. Always clean and bright and about the best mannered children in the school." I was amazed at her comments. "Thank you," I replied, " no it has not been easy and I miss my husband greatly, but my children keep me occupied."

"What I wanted to ask you is, have you ever thought about getting back into education? Now that your children are all at school there is nothing to stop you," she said. "No, it has never entered my head," I replied. "Well there is such a shortage of teachers and I am sure it wouldn't take long for you to get back into the routine of learning again, and, looking at what you were like on your school records, your chances are very good." I was really taken aback and I didn't know what to say. "Don't make a decision now," she said, " go home and think about it and let me know what you decide. I will then fill you in with what it will entail, but I need to know if it's what you want to do," she said. I thanked her from the bottom of my heart and walked back home deep in thought. I was in a daze. I put the kettle on and made myself a cup of tea and sat at the table. Just then there was a knock at the door. Who can this be I thought to myself. I got up and opened the door. Who should be standing there but Steven Bratley. "Come in Steven," I said, " what are you doing here?" I am on holiday this week, and as I am not going away I thought I'd pop round and see if there are any jobs you need doing?" "That's very kind of you," I replied, "I've just made a cup of tea, would you like one?" "Yes please, if it's no trouble," he said. So we sat and drank our tea. I looked at Steven and thought what a nice young man he was. He had a mop of blonde hair and lovely bright blue eyes, just the opposite of my Jed. He had been in the same class as Jed at school and they were exact opposites. Jed loved sport and was always full of life, but Steven was quiet, shy, and very studious.

We sat and chatted and I filled him with all my stories and he told me about his life. He still lived at home and he had had one or two girl friends but nothing serious. Then I told him about what Miss Dakin had said to me this morning. He didn't hesitate, "Go for it," he said, "it will be the best thing that could happen to you." Then he asked me if he could take me out the next day. "I will pick you up after the children have gone to school and we could have a run out into the countryside and I will bring a picnic," he said. I didn't know what to say so I started to make excuses. "Oh! please say you will come," he said, "I will have you back in time for the children coming out of school." "Alright then," I replied, "I'll be ready." After he had gone I started on my housework, my head was in a whirl. What was I thinking of, saying I would go out with Steven Bratley. But then what harm would come of it. After I had settled the children off to bed that night I felt quite excited.

The morning dawned and it was lovely and sunny. I took the children to school and went home to get ready. I only had one dress, so I carefully lifted it of its hanger and hoped it would still fit me. It was pale blue with little white flowers dotted here and there. I put it on and I knew I looked nice. I carefully did my hair and for the first time in years I put on some face cream and lipstick. I saw Steven's car pull up at the front and he came and knocked on the door. "Are you ready?" he said, and looked me up and down. "My, you look lovely," he exclaimed. We got into the car and I realised I hadn't told a soul where I was going, but then I suppose it didn't really matter. It was lovely to be in a car, this was a real treat for me.

Neither of us spoke for a while and the miles soon quickly passed. "Where are we going?" I said eventually. "Thought I would park the car up on the top of the moors and we could have a little walk if that's alright with you," said Steven. "Oh! Steven that would be lovely, I've never been out here before." The countryside was beautiful and the beginning of spring was in the air. The hedgerows were full of buds and leaves and the trees were full of blossom. I felt in awe. He parked the car and we started our walk. It all felt so unreal. We didn't need to talk and we walked for most of the morning. I had never felt so free before and when we got back to the car it was as though I was in a different world. Steven must have read my thoughts when he said, "A bit different to back home with all the pit soot and grime isn't it?"

He spread a blanket on the ground and opened the picnic basket as we sat down. I didn't realise I was so hungry, we tucked in to cheese and pickle sandwiches and hot tea from a flask followed by home made buttered scones. I did enjoy it. He talked about his plans for the future. He was studying to be a chartered accountant and said once he had passed his finals he would move away and make a new life away from the pit. We sat for a while in the lovely sunshine and I said it was time to be going home. We cleared up the picnic and walked back to the car. As we got into the car Steven held my hand. "Thank you for coming with me," he said, " you are such a lovely person Annie, and I do enjoy being with you." I felt quite embarrassed by his attention but also very flattered that I was being admired by another man especially someone as nice as Steven Bratley. We arrived home and he dropped me off at my front door. I thanked him for the lovely day we'd spent together and went in home and changed. I washed the makeup off my face and began my household chores. My head was in a whirl. I had enjoyed my day out so much and felt no guilt. My children arrived home from school and I served their tea with my head in the clouds. "Are you alright mummy," said Alison as she wiped the dishes. "Yes love," I replied, and I thought I would tell her about going out with Steven and also about what Miss Dakin had suggested. The other children had gone out to play and Joanne was sitting at the table doing her homework. I carefully explained where I had been with Steven and Alison listened intently. When I had finished my story Alison said, "Oh! Mum I am so happy for you." "So you don't mind my going then?" I answered. "No, not at all," she replied, "I'm so glad you enjoyed yourself." Unknown to me Joanne had been listening." "Good for you mum," she said, and carried on with her work. I couldn't help but smile to myself. I then explained about studying again to become a teacher. I had half made my mind up not to go ahead with the idea when Alison said, "Mum you must do it," as if by command. "Yes but," I started to say. "Never mind, yes but, you must give it a try. We will all help you and I am sure you will do well," she answered.

So the following day I found myself outside the door of Miss Dakin's office. I knocked and she invited me in. "Hello Annie do have a seat," she said. "I have come to tell you my decision," I said. "Good," she answered, "I hope you are going to go ahead with it." "Yes," I said, "I will give it a try, I have thought about what to do, but the decision was taken out of my hands by my daughters, they said I should go for it." "Good for them," she answered, "so now I will tell you what will be involved. I see you achieved good grades in your school certificate. You took nine subjects and your best grades were in English, although you obtained mostly A's in your other subjects. A talent like yours must be sustained." So she proceeded to tell me what I would have to do. I went home and sat and studied the papers she had given me. It all sounded so very exciting, but would I be able to do all this studying? There was a letter waiting for me on the mat when I got in. It was from Mary Doherty, I had written to tell her about my becoming a teacher. Her letter was full of enthusiasm and I read it through with great pleasure. Mary was now retired and back in her native Cork. She had bought a little cottage overlooking the sea. She was always inviting us to go across and see her. Just pay your fares here and I will look after you all, she used to write. Well that would have to be put on hold now, I thought to myself. I started on my daily chores and I found myself singing to myself as I hung out the washing.

Steven Bratley kept calling to see us and he was very good company. It was nice to have someone to talk to and the children enjoyed having him around. One day he suggested that we all went to the seaside. "We won't all be able to fit into your car," I said. "I've thought of that," he answered, "I thought we would go on the train." "Oh! Don't you think it would cost too much," I said. "Let me worry about that," he said. So off we went the following Saturday. The children were so excited and had never been on a train before, come to think of it neither had I, also I had never been to the seaside. We were up early that morning and the sun was shining. We caught the bus to the station and waited on the platform. I looked at my little brood all dressed in their Sunday best and felt so proud. Little Jed was jumping up and down and when the great big steam train pulled into the station, we climbed on in just a few minutes. We soon settled in and I sat with Jed and Natalie whilst Steven had Sally and Angela at his side. The two older girls sat together looking very prim and proper. I caught a glance at my eldest daughter; she was so grown up and was becoming a beautiful young lady. She had long flowing black hair and big brown eyes and I thought she would break someone's heart one day. Joanne was more like me but still had her father's lovely black hair.

The train's whistle blew and we were on our way. Soon we were speeding along and the countryside was beautiful. I looked across at Steven; he was talking to Sally and Angela and pointing to the different places we were going through. He never seemed to tire of their endless questions. I thought what a nice person he was and couldn't understand why such a lovely young man would want to be bothered with someone like me with six young children.

When we reached our destination we piled off the train. Going through the ticket barrier they never stopped talking. Soon we were on the sea front. The deep blue sea shone in the distance and the miles of sand stretched before us. What a sight to behold. I sat down on the nearest seat and my family gathered round me. "Can we go on the sands," said Jed. "Please mummy let's," said Angela. "Just wait one moment," said Steven, "we need to get some things before we go down there." So off to the shops we went. Buckets and spades and swimsuits were soon amassed and I had brought a towel with us. Packed in my bag was a load of food so now we were ready. Steven fetched us both a deck chair and we sat together whilst the children played in the sand. Gradually the tide came in and the little ones took off their shoes and socks and paddled and splashed in the water. Alison and Joanne went for a walk and when they came back we had our sandwiches. The afternoon wore on and Steven took the little ones and fetched us all an ice cream. By the time it got to teatime we knew we would have to be getting back to catch the train home. We cleared up our things and decide to have fish and chips for tea. We climbed back over the rocks on to the promenade and Steven fetched our food. We sat on the sea wall and tucked into the tastiest fish and chips I have ever had. On the train journey home the two little ones fell asleep and the others never stopped talking. I couldn't thank Steven enough and as we arrived home I took hold of his hand and as tears rolled my cheeks I thanked him from the bottom of my heart.

This had been a day we would never forget, and when the young ones were in bed Alison turned to me and said, "Mum isn't Steven a nice person and wasn't it good of him to take us away like he did." "It was my darling," I replied, "we have a lot to thank him for."

The next few weeks were so busy I didn't have time to breath. I started my studies. Two days a week I attended the local college and the rest of the time I was studying at home. The days I went to college Alison looked after the children and my mother always popped in to make sure they were alright till I came home. I soon got into the routine of learning again and found myself enjoying every minute. My tutors were good and my marks were excellent and I was so happy. The time flew quickly by and after four years of intensive learning I managed to graduate with an honours degree. My daughters were learning alongside me and we used to works for hours together at our kitchen table. All my family were growing up so quickly and each one had their different qualities. Alison wanted to teach and she had done well in her grades. Joanne preferred the sciences and decided to become a paediatrician. Sally wanted to work on a farm and Angela and Natalie were quite happy just to continue at school. But the biggest shock was my son Jed; he said he was going to work in the pit like his father. As you can imagine this came as a very upsetting shock to me. I talked to Steven about it and he said leave it to me, I will talk to him. Steven did his best but my forthright son would not listen. Apart from this one upset life was running very smoothly for me, I didn't have much money and my home was very sparse, but my children were healthy and were now very grown up. Steven explained to me that life in the pit was much better now, the miners had a much easier time than when Dad and my Jed worked there. Even though they worked hard, things were very much improved and everything was now mechanical. Try as I may I hoped he would change his mind but he wouldn't listen.

My graduation day came along and my eldest daughter accompanied me. I felt so very proud when I was handed my diploma and I knew I had to thank Miss Dakin for making this happen for me. As I arrived home that night I had the most wonderful surprise waiting for me when I walked through the door. My family had arranged a party, on the table in the kitchen was a lovely spread of food and a magnificent iced cake, but sitting in the front room I could hear voices. "Come this way mum," said Sally. As I walked through the door I could see Miss Dakin sitting in the corner, old Mr and Mrs Sutton with their son Harold, my old tormentor from my school days, my mother, Archie and my brother Edward and last but not least my dear friend, Mary Doherty. Unknown to me, my children had arranged for her to be here for my graduation day. I stood and looked at them all and I was shaking like a leaf. "Oh! what a lovely surprise," I managed to squeak, "I can't believe you are all here," and I proceeded to hug them all. Mary was the last and we fell into each others arms and we cried with happiness. "Come on mum," said Joanne, "this is no time for crying." "I know love," I said, "but what a lovely surprise this has been, it's all too much." Steven came and joined us on his way home from work and we celebrated well into the night. Miss Dakin went home early, she was very frail now, but it had been so lovely to have her here. When everyone had gone home I thanked my children for all they had done and we all hugged, laughed and cried together. When I flopped into my bed that night I thanked God for giving me so much happiness and sent my love to my Jed and wished he was here by my side.

Chapter 22

We spent the summer preparing for Alison to enter University, she had been accepted at Bristol, and, although she still wanted to teach, she had excelled in languages. I had applied for a position as English teacher at the Girl's High school and after attending a very stringent interview, found I had been chosen.

We had to thank Steven for running us backwards and forwards to Bristol and helping to settle Alison into her dormitory. He took it all in his stride and I did so love having him around. The children accepted him like part of the family, but I just felt he was like an old friend. He never talked as if there was anything between us, but I knew he cared deeply for me. I had a feeling that if I had shown any affection towards him, he would tell me he loved me, but my love was still with my Jed. I didn't want anyone else to replace him.

I started my job and soon fell into the routine of teaching, I loved every minute of my working life. The girls I taught were mature and seemed to enjoy my lessons. It was like living in a different world and when I returned home each afternoon and passed the old colliery belching out the soot and fumes, I prayed for the day when I could get us away from it all.

I made friends with quite a few of the teaching staff. Molly White, the history teacher helped me quite a lot and we became good friends. She was a year older than me and this was her second year at this school. We got together in our breaks and she kept me in touch with what was going on in school. She warned me who to steer clear of and also who I could trust. One person she pointed out was Alan Dixon, head of science. A smart young man with dark wavy hair and a lovely smile. He knew he was good looking and certainly made the most of it. He seemed to make a play for all the new lady teachers and I was no exception. "How about coming out with me tonight Annie?" he said, one day whilst I was in the staff room doing some marking. He had waited whilst I was on my own. "Sorry Alan," I said, "nothing doing, I have far too much to do at night to go out." "Some other time," he said. "No, I don't think so," I replied. "I won't give up," he answered, and he blew me a kiss as he went out of the door. I told Molly about him and she smiled and said, "Be careful." There were only two men teachers at this school. Up to four years ago only lady teachers were employed here. But gradually the times were changing and men were being accepted. The other man was Peter Drysden, a very nice middle-aged man who taught maths.

My life settled into a good routine. My daughters and my son were a great help to me and, now that they were staying for school dinners, it took a weight off me not having to start cooking when I arrived home. I spent my evenings catching up with my marking and preparing lessons, so when the school holidays came along I was usually ready for a break. So as we approached the Easter holiday I decided we would go away. I wrote to Mary in Ireland and she was overjoyed that we were going to visit her. When the day came for us to go, Steven took us to the station and as he waved goodbye I had a strange feeling in my heart and wished he was coming with us. We boarded the train and travelled to Anglesey in Wales to catch the ferry to Dublin. It was so exciting. I looked at my children's faces and they looked very bewildered and Alison and Joanne were now young women. Alison was just completing her first year at University and Joanne was about to start. Sally had left school and was working at the local vets. Angela was at technical school, she wanted to be a secretary, and Natalie was into beauty. She fancied being a beautician and wanted to work with the stars. Jed was still causing me concern. He had a lovely sunny nature and made friends easily but he was still determined to work in the pit. I had talked to him and so had Steven. Steven had even taken him over to see his dad, Tom Bratley. Tom tried to explain to him what life was like underground. He told him what the miners endured. He also explained that there wasn't much future in the coal industry. Coal was now being imported from Poland because it was much cheaper than mining in this country, but Jed didn't listen. Tom knew that pits were closing down and lots of men would be out of work. Bristow mine was on the cards so he knew that it was only a matter of time before there would be mass unemployment in our area. He had the idea that he wanted to try and understand why his father and his grandfather had been killed, and he talked about how he would change things and make life safer for the miners, but he would still be underground and facing all the perils that these poor men faced everyday. There had already been two Jed Harpers lost to the devil coal without me losing my baby.

We boarded the ferry to Dublin, our first time on a boat. The crossing was smooth and we were soon into Dublin harbour. We caught the train to Cork and as we alighted on the platform Mary was there to meet us. We went towards her and no words were needed. After the hugs and the kisses we boarded the bus to the village where she lived. We hadn't far to walk to her cottage, which was perched on the hillside overlooking the sea. It was idyllic. Mary hadn't room to sleep us all and my two eldest girls slept next door at Mary's neighbours, but we were together everyday and the weather was good to us. We spent endless hours walking on the beach and sampling some of Mary's delicious food. She wouldn't let me near to the kitchen and I felt thoroughly spoilt. My children made new friends and Mary and me spent endless time together. We talked about our lives and dreams and I told her about Steven. "Annie you have so much to give, and if Steven loves you as I am sure he does, just remember you have only one life time to live and if Steven brings you the happiness you deserve, then give him a chance." "Yes, but what about my Jed?" I answered. "I am sorry dear to be so blunt, but Jed isn't here any more and I think you should stop living in the past." Her lovely voice lilted on. When the two weeks came to an end I just did not want to return home. We had gone through so much together over the years and I cherished her as my dearest friend.

On our return home, Steven was waiting for us. He had done some shopping for me and the table was laid for tea. As I stepped out of the taxi he put his arms around me and said, "Oh! Annie it's lovely to have you home, I have missed you," and for the first time he kissed me. "I'm sorry Annie," he said, "I'm not being fair to you." "That's alright Steven," I replied, "I wanted you to kiss me," and arm in arm we walked into the house.

When Steven went home that evening I thought about what had happened and I felt guilty. The children were tired and were soon off to their beds. Joanne had gone to see one of her friends and Alison came and sat with me as I stared into the glowing embers of the fire. "What's wrong mum?" she said. "Nothing love," I answered. "You can't fool me," she replied, "come on, tell me what's bothering you?" and she sat at the side of me and took my hand in hers. "Oh! love I feel so guilty," I said, as tears came into my eyes. "But why mum, you have nothing to feel guilty about," she answered. "Yes but I am getting too fond of Steven and just now when we arrived home he kissed me, and the thing is I wanted to kiss him back," I rambled on. "Mother you have every right to kiss Steven, its time you two got together. He's been very patient waiting for you all these years," she said. "But I still love your dad," I answered. "Yes, but dad isn't here and you're still young, it's time you made a new life for yourself. We won't be around for ever and you can tell Steven loves you." What a speech from my lovely daughter. "Well love I'll sleep on it," I said, "I'll remember what you have said and see how I feel tomorrow," and went up to my bed. I soon fell into a deep restful sleep and next morning felt at peace with the world. After lunch I heard Steven's car stop at the front door. I was busy washing up and I dried my hands and went to greet him. "Hello, Steven," I said, "Do come in." He followed me through into the kitchen. I thought how nice he looked. He was wearing grey slacks and open necked blue shirt. "Annie," he said, "I've come to apologise." "You've nothing to apologise for," I answered, "I wanted you to kiss me." "You did?" he said and looked amazed. He came over and put his arms around me. "Oh! my darling Annie, I love you so very much," he said, " I've loved you for such a long time but never thought I stood a chance," and as we stood together our hearts seem to beat as one. "I love you Steven," I said and meant it with all of my heart.

Chapter 23

The school holidays came to an end and I returned to teaching again. My two elder daughters were away, Alison had taken a teaching job at a college in Manchester. Her subject was French, for which she had received an Honours degree. Joanne was in London beginning her training as a paediatrician. Sally was still working for Mr Whitworth the local vet. Angela was now a secretary working for the National Coal Board. Natalie was training to be a hairdresser and often experimented on her sisters and me. My son, Jed had gone into the pit. His first year was at a training school and spent part of the time working underground. For this I wasn't very pleased.

The relationship I had with Steven was progressing very slowly. I was still very unsure about him. He was a lovely person but I knew in my heart I would never love him as I had loved my Jed.

We had quite a few new members of staff as the number of children had increased. Helping me was a sweet young girl just out of college, her name was Beverley Davies. She was very bright and soon settled in to the school routine. She was a great help to me and once or twice I took her back to my home. She was always very interested in the stories I told her about the pit and the life I had led as a child. She would listen for hours as I told her what life was like in the air raid shelters in the war, how the men suffered in the pits and all the hardships they endured.

She told me of her life and how her mother had died when she was only six years old. Her father was a bank manager and her grandparents had brought her up. One day she invited me to go to her house to meet her father. I had to tell Steven not to come round. He had got into the habit of coming to see me most nights. Although he was still very attentive I found myself holding back from making any commitment to him.

John Davies was waiting for me at the door as I arrived. Beverley introduced us and as I shook hands with this tall majestic looking man, my heart missed a beat. "Welcome to my home Mrs Harper," he said, "I have heard so much about you." "Thank you," I replied, "but please call me Annie." He ushered me into the sitting room. It was a lovely room with thick carpet and deep comfy chairs. I perched on the edge of the settee and Beverley offered me a glass of sherry. John Davies came to sit beside me and I was very impressed by this handsome man. "I want to thank you so much for the help you have given my daughter," he said, "she is always so full of praise for you." "Well thank you," I replied, "but honestly she is the one who has been helping me." "Beverley is always talking about you," he continued, "you must have had a struggle to bring up all your children, I hope life is a bit easier for you now." "Yes it hasn't always been easy but my children have been wonderful and I have a lot to be grateful for," I replied. Just then Beverley called and said it was time to eat. John escorted me through into the dining room. This room was light and airy and Beverley had gone to quite a lot of trouble to put on a nice meal for us. Throughout the meal we chatted like old friends and I found myself warming to this lovely man. He had bright blue eyes and dark hair and a lovely warm smile lit up his face. When we had finished eating I offered to clear up but Beverley wouldn't hear of it and told us to go and sit out on the balcony and she would bring coffee. It was a lovely evening and as we sat together looking over the beautiful gardens, I couldn't help but think how lucky I was to have come this far. The evening passed and I had enjoyed myself so much. John offered to run me home in his car. Sitting beside him as he carefully drove I glanced at his profile and I thought what a gentle man he was. He walked me to my front door and I thanked him for a lovely evening. "We must do it again sometime," he said as he drove off. When I got in Sally and Natalie were in bed, Angela was ironing, and Jed was dozing in front of the fire. "Hello son," I said, "are you alright?" "Yes mother," he answered. "Why don't you go to bed if you are so tired," I asked. "He wants to tell you what he's been doing," said Angela. "Oh! shut up our Angela," Jed said. I walked over to Jed and put my arms around him. "What's wrong love, come on tell your Mum," I said. "I've been down the pit today," replied Jed. I knew this was the first time and I wondered how he would react. "Well then what did you think?" "Oh! mum it was unbelievable," he replied, "how the poor men exist in those conditions I will never know. Do you know mum some of the men were working knee deep in water and the water was still seeping in, it was awful." "It hasn't put you off then?" I asked. "No, not really. I just want to make things better for them." "But how can you do that?" I answered. "I wish I could make things safer for them and working conditions much better, I would also like to see a better wage for miners and shorter shifts," he said. "Look love, this would take a lot of sorting out," I said. "Yes, but I am sure I could come up with some ideas," he replied. "Well why not sleep on it my darling you look really tired," and I gave him a kiss and he went up to bed.

Angela put the ironing board away and I made us both some cocoa. "He has some bright ideas doesn't he mum?" she said. "Yes, he does and they are all good ones," I replied. "Have you enjoyed your evening?" she said. "Oh! yes," I answered and proceeded to tell her about John Davies and his lovely home. "Do you think you will see him again?" she asked. "Probably love," I answered, "but I can't very well bring him back here can I?" "Why not?" said Angela, "if he's as nice as you say he is I'm sure he won't mind where you live," and with that she went to bed. I sat and stared into the fire and I thought about the handsome John Davies and I knew deep inside I would dearly love to see him again.

The next day at school I did not see Beverley till lunchtime. She had been working on a different project that was nothing to do with me but we sat and had lunch together. I thanked her once again for the lovely meal she had prepared and she informed me how very impressed her father had been with my company. I felt very flattered. Two weeks passed by and in that time my son had been down the pit three more times and each time he was convinced he could make life easier for the miners. Then I received a phone call from John Davies. He rang me during lunch break and after we had discussed various topics he asked me if I would like to go to the theatre with him. "I've got tickets for Macbeth at the Alhambra for Thursday night," he said. "I would love to come," I replied. So it was arranged that he would pick me up at seven on Thursday evening.

I was tingling with excitement as I waited for his arrival. If I looked into the mirror once I must have looked a hundred times. "Oh! mum you look lovely," said Natalie. She made up my face, painted my nails, and set my hair. I was wearing my new blue suit and felt like a queen. Then I saw his car pull up at the front gate. My mouth felt dry and I was very nervous. He knocked on the door and soon I settled in his car. As we drove away I saw Steven's car coming down the road, I had told him I was going out but he must have forgotten. I turned round sharply and John said, "Anything wrong Annie?" "No, it's alright John," I replied, "I just saw someone I know." "Do you want me to stop," he said. "No, keep going," I replied. We drove to the theatre and John found me a place to sit. He brought across two glasses of sherry and came and sat beside me. "You look lovely tonight Annie," he said and squeezed my hand. "Thank you," I replied and felt very tongue-tied. We found our seats on the front row of the gallery and watched a wonderful production of Macbeth. I had never been to anything like this before, I was enjoying myself so much, and John presented me with a box of chocolates. When the show was over we went out into the night, and walked along in the moonlight my arm placed gently in his. It was just so nice being together. We reached the car and John opened the door and helped me in. "Thank you so much," I said. "But the evening isn't over yet," he announced. "Why! Where are we going?" I asked. "Do you fancy a bite to eat?" he questioned. "That would be nice," I said. He drove out into the countryside to a lovely hotel and we were shown to a table for two in the corner of this magnificent room. John asked me to choose the wine I would like to drink and the menu was brought to us. We selected our food and dined and drank our wine, I felt so at peace with the world. Then he drove me home, and when we reached my house I thanked John over and over again for the wonderful evening we had spent together. "It is I who should be thanking you," he said, " I have so much enjoyed your company." He opened the car door and helped me out. "Goodnight my dear," he said and briefly brushed my cheek with his kiss. Then he was gone.

The house was in darkness as I let myself in. I looked at the clock, it was two-fifteen, my goodness I will never get up in the morning, I thought to myself. I washed off my make up and climbed into bed but sleep evaded me. I was reliving my wonderful evening thinking of the happiness John had brought me.

Next day the girls in my class seemed extra boisterous or was it me just feeling tired. The day seemed to drag on forever and I was glad it was the weekend. Alison was coming home for the weekend and I was so looking forward to seeing her. I did some shopping on my way home from school and I was meeting Alison at the station at nine-fifteen. Whilst I was putting my shopping away and generally tidying round, Steven arrived. "Hello Steven," I said as he walked into the kitchen, "it's lovely to see you." Steven looked very serious; his usual smiling face was gone. "Oh! Hello Annie," he muttered and slumped into the nearest chair. "Anything wrong?" I asked. "No, everything is fine," he answered. "Well you don't look very happy, are you ill or something?" I went on. "No, I've told you everything is fine. I just wondered if you would like me to run you to the station to meet Alison that's all?" he snapped. "That would be nice," I answered. "Sure my car is good enough for you to ride in?" he said. "Why ever not?" I replied. "Oh! I thought you preferred something better," he said. "That's an awful thing to say, you know I love to ride in your car," I answered. "Right then I'll come round later on and take you, let's see did you say the train gets in at nine-fifteen?" he queried. "Yes it does, but won't you stay and have some tea with me I'm just about to make a sandwich," I said. "No thank you I've got things to do so I'll see you later," he replied, and he let himself out of the door.

"Who was that mum," said Natalie coming down stairs, "I heard the door slam." "It was Steven," I replied. "What's wrong with him and why isn't he staying for tea?" she went on. "I don't know love, he seems in a right old mood," I said. "Don't you realise he's jealous?" she smiled. "What has he to be jealous about?" I queried. "Surely mother you must know, he doesn't like you going out with your Mr Davies," she laughed. "That is silly Natalie, he's nothing to be jealous about," I replied, and proceeded to make the tea. My thoughts were far away and wondered if there was some truth in Steven's behaviour. I got myself ready and Steven came at eight-thirty, we drove to the station in silence. "I'll wait in the car till the train comes in," he said. "Don't be silly I want you there with me," I replied. "You don't need me," he said and turned his head away. "But of course I want you with me Steven, please come and meet Alison off the train." "Oh! alright," he said and reluctantly got of the car. The train arrived and my lovely daughter alighted on to the platform. She came towards me and gave me a hug. "Hello mum," she said, " it's lovely to see you." I held her close and tears rolled down my cheeks. "Now come on mum, there's no need for tears," she said and turned to Steven and gave him a hug. On the way home we never stopped talking and I invited Steven to join us, but he said he wanted to go home. When we went in the house there were hugs and kisses from her sisters, Jed took a back seat until he had the chance to get a word in. "Oh! Jed how you've changed," said Alison, "you look so grown up." "Well I am a working man now," replied Jed, "not just a namby pamby school boy." I stared at my wonderful son and thought how like his father he was. About six feet tall with his mop of black hair, and I felt so upset when I thought how much my lovely Jed had missed with his untimely death. I excused myself and went to the bathroom. I sat on the edge of the bath and sobbed till I thought my heart would break. "Are you in there mum?", I heard Alison's voice. "I'm coming love just give me a minute," I answered. I rinsed my face and went to join my family.

The next day Alison and me went shopping. It was good to have her with me. We both bought new clothes and had our lunch at a smart cafe. Whilst the waiter brought our coffee Alison told me about her life and how she loved her job. She had also met a young man and seemed besotted with him. She was now twenty-two and had a very sensible head on her shoulders. She asked how things were progressing with Steven and when I told her about John Davies her face lit up. "But mother what are you going to do?" she asked. "I don't know," I replied, "I think the world of Steven but I do enjoy being with John." "You don't have to make a decision yet," she said, "why don't you wait and see how things go." "You're right," I answered, "but I can't bear to see Steven so miserable."

That night all my girls went out together. Jed was round at his friend's house so I thought I would get on with some jobs. I had a lot of washing to do and work to set for Monday morning. I had just settled down with a nice cup of coffee when I saw a car pull up at the front of the house. My goodness its John's car and I jumped up quickly and spilt my coffee all over the carpet. He knocked on the door and I went to open it. "Hello John," I said, "what are you doing here?" "Forgive me Annie, I hope you don't mind me calling round so unexpected, but I wondered if you would like to go out for a run somewhere?" he replied, "I would have rung you if you had a telephone, but I suddenly thought I would like to see you." I felt myself shaking and invited him in to my shabby sitting room. "Please sit down John," I said, "just excuse me a minute I have spilt my coffee and I must mop it up." I went into the kitchen and fetched a cloth. I felt so unglamorous down on my knees mopping up coffee. "Would you like me to go?" he said. "No," I answered, "just let me clear this mess up and then I will be with you." I rinsed the cloth and then went back into the sitting room. John looked gorgeous in his dark blue slacks and white shirt. "I'm sorry for all this mess," I stuttered, and started to clear up my books. "No it's me who should be sorry," he said, "taking you by surprise like this, but it was such a lovely evening I thought we could go out for a run." "If you don't mind waiting while I get changed," I said, "I would love to come out with you."

I quickly went upstairs to get ready. I knew there was no chance of Steven coming round because he said he would let us have a family weekend together. I put on my new white blouse and floral skirt, which I had bought that morning, and with a quick spot of powder and lipstick I was ready. I left a note for my girls and with John's help climbed into his car. He turned to me and smiled, "You do look lovely," he said and off we went. I felt so grand sitting there in this lovely luxury car and he asked me how Alison was and we chatted away like old friends. I soon relaxed in his company.

He must have read my thoughts for I was about to ask him where we were going when he said, "I thought we would have a run to Rickworth Park and perhaps have a little walk and maybe supper later if that's alright with you." "Oh! that would be lovely John," I replied. I had not been to Rickworth Park before but I had heard about its lovely stately home and beautiful gardens. We chatted amiably as we drove along and soon reached our destination. It was a lovely evening with a faint breeze blowing. John parked the car and we began our walk through the winding paths that took us down by the riverbank. We sauntered through beautiful Hydrangea bushes till we came to the gardens, the flowerbeds were a magnificent blaze of colour and the scent from the flowers mingled with the masculine smell of John's aftershave. "Would you like to sit a while Annie?" John asked and we found the nearest bench and sat and enjoyed the peaceful scene before us. We chatted about our everyday lives and John filled me in on his early childhood. It was so different to the life I had led. His father had been in the army and they had travelled the world. He had one brother, Charles, who now lived in Australia. His parents John and Hilda lived in Devon and were quite elderly. He told me about his wife Linda and the terrible suffering she had endured with heart problems, and what a joy his daughter Beverley was. He had never found anyone to replace Linda and had put all his energy into looking after Beverley with the help of Linda's parents, and how his job had kept him sane. He asked me about my life and I found it so easy to talk to John. It brought back the memories of the life I'd had, I told him about my Grandma Pointer, my lovely Grandma Clayton, my mother and father and the terrible conditions in the pit. The love I had for Jed and the struggles I had endured. He listened intently and when I told him about my Jed's untimely death I was soon in tears. John put his arms around me and let me sob. "I am so sorry," I said, "I didn't mean this to happen." "Don't worry my dear," he said, "I'm sorry I have upset you." "Oh! but you haven't," I answered, "I'm just being silly." He held me close and I felt so much comfort in his arms.

We drove home through a moonlit night and we decided to go straight home. Neither of us felt like eating. "Good night Annie," he said, and put his arms around me, "thank you for a lovely evening," and then he kissed me. My heart went out to this lovely man as I accepted his kiss and said, "Good night."

My mind was in a turmoil as I let myself in. The house was empty, for which I was pleased. I screwed up the note I had left for my girls and made my way up to bed. It didn't take long to fall into a luxurious sleep still feeling John Davies's arms around me.

Next day I told my daughters about my outing to Rickworth Park and they listened with quiet contentment. Jed came barging in and picked up snatches of our conversation. "Good for you mum," he said, "you do right to enjoy yourself," and to this comment my daughters agreed. That afternoon Steven came round to take Alison to the station, he looked so down and my heart went out to him. After we had waved goodbye to Alison we returned to the car. Steven started up the ignition and soon we were on our way back home. Steven didn't speak. When we reached my house I said, "Are you coming in Steven?" "No, I'll get off home," he said, "You must have work to do." I thought about the books I still had to mark, but I couldn't let him go like this. "Oh! please come in and have a cup of tea," I said. "Are you sure I won't be in the way?" he queried. "Of course not Steven I am always pleased to have your company." "Ok then I'll park the car." He took the car round to the back of the house and I put the kettle on. Steven came into the kitchen. "How have you been these last few days?" he said, "I don't seem to have seen much of you." "Fine, Steven," I replied, "it's been lovely to have Alison at home, how are you?" "Not too bad Annie, but I have missed you. Mind you I've been very busy and my dad hasn't been too well," he replied. "Oh! dear what has been wrong with him?" I asked. "Just the usual trouble," he said, "his chest and lungs are getting worse." "I am so sorry Steven, I've always thought a lot about your dad, he did some good work in the pit," I answered. "Yes, this is why he's suffering now," he answered forlornly. I poured the tea and we went into the front room and sat side by side on the settee. I told him about the work Jed was doing and he listened intently, I said how worried I was about him but there was nothing I could do. "Best let him get on with it," said Steven, "he will make his own mistakes." "Yes, but he is so young and I don't want him working underground. He seems to think he can make great changes in the working conditions but I don't think things will ever change. Mining will always be a hazardous job," I said. "Would you like me to have a word with him?" said Steven. "Well you could but it won't make much difference," I replied, "anyway how is your job, still keeping busy?" "Most certainly, I am doing so well I'm thinking of buying my own house," he said. "My goodness, Steven that is a big undertaking," I said with alarm in my voice. "Yes, I have given it a lot of thought and I know I can afford it," he replied, "I wondered if you would come with me to help me choose a place when you've the time. I thought we could go to the estate agents and have a look together." "That would be lovely Steven," I replied, "just let me know, and we can arrange something." "Oh! thank you Annie, it would make me happy to have you with me," he answered, and he put his arms around me and held me so close I could hardly breathe. "Annie I love you so very much," he said, and he kissed me. I returned his kiss and my heart went out to him. When he had gone my mind was in a turmoil. What was I going to do? My feelings for Steven were so genuine and true, but John held my heart in his hands. Still the feeling of guilt was with me because my real love was the man I had buried all those years ago, my lovely husband, and father of my children, my Jed.

A week passed by and I was so busy at school. We were doing preparatory work before the exams. I didn't hear from either Steven or John and in some ways I was pleased, it gave me the chance to try and sort out in my mind where my destiny lay. Then John rang me at work and invited me over to his place for a meal. When I arrived the table was laid with some lovely cold food and John greeted me with open arms. "It's lovely to see you Annie," he said, "I haven't been in touch before because Beverley told me how busy you were at school." "That's right John," I replied, "it has been pretty hectic." "Help yourself to food," he said, "and I thought we could sit out on the veranda and eat." "That's a good idea," I said. He handed me a plate and I helped myself to salad and ham and a chunk of crusty bread and went out on to the veranda. John followed me and he poured me glass of lovely clear cold wine. The evening was cool and we sat in silence whilst we ate our food. "John this is lovely," I said. "Yes it's good to have you here," he answered, "I have missed you." We sat and chatted till I felt chilly. "Let's go indoors," he said and we went into his beautiful sitting room and he turned on the electric fire and came and sat beside me. "You must realise Annie I am becoming very fond of you," he said and snuggled up to me. "I love being with you and when you are away I miss you so much. I do hope I'm not rushing things Annie, and please forgive me if you do not return my affections." "Oh! John I don't know what to say, you see I love being with you but I still love my Jed. I know it's been a long time but I swore when he died I would never let another man into my life, and so far I have been happy as things are," I answered. "I knew I was being presumptuous," he said and moved away from me. "Just give me time," I said, "I am very fond of you John." We spent the evening talking and listening to music and when it was time to go home John apologised for his outburst earlier on. I told him not to worry and thanked him for a very pleasant evening. He took me home and escorted me to my front door. His goodnight kiss fell lightly on my lips. "Goodnight Annie," he said, "I do hope I haven't upset you." I let myself in and my heart was beating fast.

The following day as I arrived home from work, Steven's car was parked at my house. When I went in he was sitting at the kitchen table drinking tea and talking to Jed. "Hello," I said, "how's every one?" "Hello mum," said Jed, "Steven is trying to make me change my mind about working underground, aren't you Steven?" "No! I'm only offering you advice," said Steven, "I've seen the misery and suffering the miners have endured and I wouldn't want you to suffer the same." "Yes, but it will be different for me," said Jed, "I aim to make the conditions in the pit safer and I am learning so much at college and besides it's so different in the mines these days. Being underground isn't like it used to be, everything is much more modern." "Yes, but you are still underground," said Steven, "and accidents can still happen." "But accidents can happen in every job," replied my defiant son. "It's no good Steven," I said, "I have gone through all this with him, so you might as well save your breath." "But mum," said my forthright son. "Never mind, but mum," I replied, "you try and take notice of what Steven is saying to you." "OK I will listen but I still have my own ideas," he said. With that he went off to his friend's house. "I'm so sorry Steven," I said, "but thanks for trying." "Well I did my best," he said, "but he is still very young and we all made mistakes at his age." Steven was so very understanding and my feelings for him so strong but still I could not commit myself. "Stay and have a bite to eat with us," I said. "Well that would be nice, I was just on my way home," he said. "Perhaps after tea you could take me to see your dad," I said, "I would love to see him again." "That's a good idea," replied Steven, "I'm sure he would be pleased to see you." "I cut into the cold meat left over from Sunday's joint and made us some sandwiches. When we had finished I left a note for my girls telling them what to have for their teas and where I had gone. We were soon on our way. "Don't be too upset when you see my dad Annie, will you? He looks so ill," said Steven, as he carefully drove the car. "I'll try not to be," I replied. Arriving at Steven's parents' home he pushed open the back door and said, "It's only me and I've got a surprise for you." I followed Steven into the pristine kitchen. Mrs Bratley was washing up. "Hello Steven," she said. "Look who I've brought Mum," he said, and Mrs

Bratley turned towards me wiping her hands on the kitchen towel. "My goodness, it's Annie Clayton," she said, "Oh! what a lovely surprise." She came towards me and put her arms around me. "My! Annie you haven't changed a bit," she said, "it's such a long time since I saw you." "Hello! Mrs Bratley," I answered, "it's lovely to see you too. I'm so sorry I haven't been to see you but I have been so busy." "You'll have enough on your plate without coming round here," she said, "what with your job and your family. How are you all keeping?" "Oh! we are coping alright," I replied. "It must have been hard for you Annie, but you have done so well, managing to hold down a teaching job and bring up your family. How are they all and what are they doing?" she said. I filled her in with all my news. I told her how my daughters were progressing and then I told her about Jed. "Yes, Steven told me he had gone in the pit," she said. "That must have been a shock to you my dear." "It certainly was," said Steven, "I've just been trying to talk some sense into him." "Never mind," said Vera Bratley, "you can only stand by and be there for him. I'll put the kettle on." " How's dad today?" said Steven. "He's had a better day and seems a bit brighter," said Mrs Bratley, "take Annie through to see him, he will be so pleased to have a visitor, and I will make us a cup of tea."

Steven ushered me into to the front room. "Hello! Dad," he said, "how are you today? I've brought someone to see you." His dad was sitting near the window reading a book. He looked up. "Hello son," he said, and he closed his book and got up from his chair and gave Steven a hug. "And who is this?" he said, "my goodness it's Annie Clayton." He came to where I was standing and put his arms around me. "My goodness Annie this is a lovely surprise," he said, "do sit down." I looked at this frail old man, who by now was struggling to get his breath, and my thoughts went back to when I was small and my mother had taken me to the pit whilst the miners were being rescued and how I had snuggled up to Grandma Clayton while the snow fell around us. This brave man had worked tirelessly to save those miners lives. I felt a lump come in my throat and leaned on Steven as I sat on the settee. The moment was broken when Vera Clayton came in with the tray of tea. She busily poured us all a cup and I looked at Tom Bratley's face as he was trying to catch his breath. He looked so old and tired but still had a twinkle in his eyes. We sat and reminisced all evening and I wondered why I had left it so long to come and visit this dear old couple. He told me stories about my dad, some things I had never heard before and I revelled in his remarkable memory. When it was time to go, I hugged

Tom Bratley and thanked him for a lovely evening. He hugged me and said, "Don't be long before you come again lass, I have enjoyed your company." As we said goodbye I glanced down at the book he had been reading. The title was 'Working in the coalmines. What the miners endured.'

Chapter 24

When I got home from school the following day there was a letter waiting for me from Mary Doherty. I knew it was my turn to write so I was quite surprised to hear from her. It was her usual newsy letter and then she suggested I go over and visit her. 'Why not come on your own' she wrote, 'it would do you good to have a break, and I am sure the family are old enough to look after themselves.' What a lovely idea, I thought, I will ask my family and see what reaction I would get. I approached them all and my girls were very enthusiastic but Jed could only think of who was going to do his packed lunches for him. "Don't worry about Jed mother," said Natalie, "I will take care of him." "Yes! don't worry," said Angela, "we will be alright." So I felt very excited about having a holiday on my own and wrote back to Mary straight away.

We broke up for the summer holidays the following week and I booked my journey to Ireland. I made sure my family were well catered for and packed my case ready for the journey. Steven said he would take me to the train and soon the day approached. I gave my family last minute instructions, and Natalie said, "We will be alright mother, stop worrying." Steven came to pick me up and waited on the station whilst my train approached. "Take care Annie," he said, "I wish I was coming with you," and kissed me tenderly on the lips. "Goodbye, Steven," I said as I returned his kiss.

It seemed strange travelling on my own, but I felt quite at peace with my world. Whatever my feelings were for Steven and John was not a worry to me. I knew it would sort itself out one way or the other. Right now this holiday was for me and I was going to relax and enjoy it.

The journey passed without a hitch and Mary was waiting for me when I arrived in Dublin. It was lovely to see her again and, although she was looking old and frail, she still had a spring in her step.

We clung together for what seemed an age, and it was lovely to be with her again. We didn't need to speak, we both knew our feelings were very deep. Once we did start talking, we never stopped. Mary's lovely Irish lilt compared to my deep Yorkshire tones. When we reached Mary's cottage not a thing had changed. The view to the sea from my bedroom window, the smell of the Wisteria growing up the cottage walls and the lovely fresh air still prevailed.

Mary had laid the table and we sat and ate her special pies and cakes. "Oh! Mary it's so lovely to be here," I said, and we sat outside in the sunshine till the evening shadows fell. This was going to be two weeks of bliss and I was going to enjoy every minute of it.

We decided to spend the first few day's just relaxing and taking walks on the beach. After I had been there two days I was really beginning to unwind when Mary said to me, "What's bothering you Annie?" "Why nothing," I replied. "There is something on your mind, I can tell," she went on, "You can't fool me." "Oh! Mary you are a canny old so and so," I said, "you don't miss a thing." "Then there is something," she replied. I proceeded to tell her about Steven and John and she listened intently. "But you must know whether you love either of them," she said. "That's just it," I said, "I don't really know how I feel." "Then there is no problem," she lilted on, "You would know if you were really in love." She was so wise this lovely old lady, but I couldn't help but wonder how she had such knowledge about being in love when she had never married. "But what do I do in the meantime?" I asked. "Just let things go and don't rush into anything," she said, " your heart will lead you to your destiny." "In the meantime enjoy being with both of them." So I decided to relax and enjoy my holiday and forget about Steven and John for the time being.

The rest of the two weeks we managed to visit some of the lovely places in County Wicklow. Mary had lots of friends and they all greeted me as if they had known me for ever. Their hospitality was superb and when it was time for me to pack my suitcase and head for home, I was more than a little sad. Mary saw me to the station and we said our goodbyes as we clung to each other, knowing this may be the last time we would be together.

On my return home, dear old Steven was waiting for me at the station. "I knew what time your train arrived," he said, as he linked my arm through his and took my suitcase firmly in his other hand. "Thank you for coming Steven," I said, "it's good to see you, how's everybody?" "Everyone is alright," he said, " but we have all missed you. Have you enjoyed yourself?" "Oh! it's been a lovely holiday Steven, I have had such a nice rest," I replied. We climbed into his car and he deftly drove through the familiar streets to my home. My family were waiting for me and there were hugs and kisses from everyone. Jed put his arms around me and said, "It's lovely to have you home mum," and I knew my big grown up son had really missed me.

I decided to spend the few weeks remaining of my school holidays doing some cleaning in the house. Jed's room needed decorating and we went together and chose paper and paint. I made a start and whilst I was tidying Jed's books and papers away I came across some of his course work from college. I sat on the edge of his bed and tried to understand some of the drawings and graphs he had done. His work was immaculate and I began to understand his enthusiasm for changes in the underground workings. This was fascinating reading and I was amazed at his knowledge. The comments from his tutor were highly praising and, at last I began to understand my son's enthusiasm for trying to make life easier for the miners. There was no way I understood the complicated drawings but I knew from now on I would be a little bit more tolerant of my sons chosen profession.

The rest of the school holidays passed so quickly and it soon came round for me to return to work. I had been so busy and my house was looking immaculate. My daughters were busy in their own work and Alison had brought her boy friend, David Sumner, home to meet me. He was a very nice person and seemed to think the world of Alison. Joanne was busy taking her final exams and was soon to become a qualified paediatrician. Sally was still working at the local vets and had a wide circle of friends. Angela worked for the N.C.B. and was now a secretary to the pit manager, while Natalie still practised on us all with her make up skills. I hadn't seen anything of John during the holiday. He had gone away to his holiday home in the south of France with Beverley for three weeks and Steven had a lot of work to do. He knew I was busy decorating the house, so he was very good and kept away. When I did see him he talked endlessly about buying his own house.

The day came for starting back at school. Not only was Beverley still with me but also a new young lady had joined our department. Her name was Hilary Spencer and she soon settled in to our routine. One morning during my break, I was called to the head teacher's office. I wondered what she needed to see me for. I tapped on her door and she called me to go in. "Do sit down," she said. "You will be wondering why I've sent for you." "Well yes," I replied as I sat opposite her. "I am putting your name forward as head of English," she continued, "you will appreciate the position will have to be advertised, but I would like to think you would be interested in this opportunity." I felt very honoured to be asked to take this position and I thanked Beryl Thompson, our good but quite remote Head teacher, for this chance. I looked around the room as I stood up and thought back to the day when I was sixteen years old and I was here with my mother to tell the then head teacher, Miss Rhodes that I was pregnant and would have to leave school. So much had happened since then and, as I thanked Mrs Thompson once again I felt a lump in my throat and I had to hide the tears as I left her room.

My family were very pleased to hear my good news and Steven came round for tea that night, we sat and talked about what the future held for us. He asked me if I would go that weekend to look at houses and I said of course I would. I filled in my application form for the position of head of English and handed it in with all my credentials to Mrs Thompson. The following day Steven and I went into town to the estate agents. We picked out quite a few houses which appealed to Steven and were within his price range. I really enjoyed being with him and looking round these lovely houses made it a pleasurable day. Then we found it, a most delightful four bed roomed house, just a nice distance out of town. It stood in it's own grounds and the garden was immaculate. We felt very excited and as we drove back to the estate agents, Steven stopped the car and pulled over to the side of the road. We were out in the lovely country side and as he stopped the car I said, "Why are we stopping?" He carefully manoeuvred the car and turned to me. He reached out and held my hand, "Annie, my darling, I want to ask you if you will marry me?" he said, "I have loved you for such a long time and I know I can give you the happiness you deserve." I turned towards his pleading face and I didn't know what to say. "Don't give me an answer right away," he said, "I would like you to think things over first, but I would love you to say yes." "Oh! Steven," "you mean so much to me," I replied, "but I will never love anyone as I loved my Jed." "I've enough love for both of us," he said, "and I can give you so much happiness and take care of you for ever. Lets go back to the estate agents and put an offer on that lovely house." With that he started up the car and we drove back into town.

When I arrived home the house was in darkness, my family were all out. Steven walked me to my door and I asked him to come in and have a cup of tea. "No, I will go now," he said. "I've taken up too much of your time today." I turned towards him and kissed his cheek and let myself into the house. My mind was in a turmoil, even though I expected Steven to propose one day, I felt very confused. I put the kettle on and made myself a cup of tea. I sat in the front room and tried to put my thoughts together when in walked Sally and Angela. They had been to the pictures. "Hello mum," they chorused, "had a good day?" "Yes thank you," I replied, "there's tea in the pot if you want a drink." They came and sat with me and told me about the film they had been to see. I sat and listened, pleased to have my mind occupied with other thoughts. "Did Steven manage to find a house he liked?" asked Sally. "As a matter of fact he did," I replied, "he has put in an offer for a lovely house up on Ridley Moor." "Good heavens mum it's lovely up there," said Angela, "I do hope he gets it." "What are his chances?" said Sally. "Well he's put in a good offer so I am sure he stands a chance," I replied. My voice must have sounded a bit flat because Angela picked up on it. "Anything wrong mum?" she said. "No love, I'm just a bit tired that's all," I answered, "but I feel very excited for Steven. If he gets that house I'm sure he'll be very happy." "He'd be happier still if you were to marry him and go and live there," chirped Sally. "Oh! Sally that's not being fair to mum," piped up Angela with a big smile on her face, she came and\squeezed in the chair besides me. I didn't know what to say as I put my arm around her shoulders. Shall I tell them about Steven's proposal of marriage, I thought, but then I didn't know what my answer was going to be. I quickly decide to leave it for a while and perhaps give myself time to think things through, so I changed the subject. I had a very restless night as I thought about Steven, I did really love him, but were my feelings deep enough to marry him? He had been part of my life for so long and I knew I couldn't keep him waiting too long for my answer.

The next day I gathered my brood together. Jed was in his room listening to his gramophone records, he wondered why I wanted to talk to him. We all gathered in the front room, Natalie with her hair in curlers, Angela wearing a facemask and Sally with her finger and toe nails painted bright red. Jed was sulking and he said, "What's going on mum?" I'm going up to Richard's house in five minutes." "You can stay where you are young man," I answered in no uncertain terms. "I have something to tell you all." They all looked up to me and I looked at my lovely family and thought how lucky I was to have such nice kids, which belonged to my Jed and me. He would never be far away from me while they were around. "What is it mum? said Sally. "Well it's like this, Steven Bratley has asked me to marry him, and I am thinking of accepting his proposal," I said. I couldn't believe I'd said these words because I was still a bit unsure and I didn't know why. My three girls came towards me and Natalie was in tears. "Oh! mum that would be lovely," they chorused. Natalie put her arms around me and we all cried together. Jed stood aside, his face was set. "I don't know how you can think of such a thing," he shouted, "what about my dad, don't you ever think about him?" and ran out of the room. I pulled myself away from my daughters and went after him, by now he was out of the house and down the back lane. I tried to run after him but there was no way I could keep up. My girls were behind me and we shouted for him to come back but he just kept on running. We returned to our house and I was shaking. Now I knew why I couldn't marry Steven Bratley.

Everything was very subdued in our house for the next few days. We tried to carry on as normal and my daughters told me to ignore their brother, but I knew I had to make my peace with him. A few days passed and I waited until I had the chance for us to have a talk. I came home from school one night and went to his room. I tapped on the door and went in, he was doing his homework. He looked up and said, "Hello mum." "Hello son," I replied, "have you time to talk?" "There's not much to talk about is there?" he said, "you have made your mind up to marry that man and you don't care about how I feel, do you, and what about my dad?" "Oh! Jed, that's not being fair," I said, "of course I care how you feel and no, I will never stop loving your father. He was the most precious person in my life, but he's been gone a long time now, and I really care for Steven. I know we could be happy, but if you don't want me to marry him then I will tell him, no." He turned to me and his face lit up. "Mum, I am so glad," he said, "I just don't want our lives to change, that's all." He turned back to his books, as far as he was concerned that was the end of the matter. I got up and left the room. As I walked down the stairs he called after me "When will tea be ready, I'm going up to Richards soon?" I was so upset as I started to prepare tea. My daughters arrived home from work and we all sat down and ate our food. Jed jumped up from the table still eating and said, "Right I'm off up to Richards now, see you!" and with that he was gone. Sally began to clear the table and Angela turned to me. "Mum are you alright?" she said. "Yes love," I answered, "I might as well tell you all I have decided not to marry Steven after all." They all stopped what they were doing. "But mum you must marry him," said Angela, "why have you changed your mind?" "It's Jed, isn't it?" said Natalie. "Let's put it this way," I said, "he doesn't want me to marry him, and unless you all give me your blessing to this marriage I won't go through with it." "But it's time you thought about yourself," said Sally, "you've every right to marry Steven, never mind what Jed thinks, he's just a selfish, mean person." "Well for the time being I will not hear any more about it, do you understand?" I said. "Yes, mother," said Sally, but I think you are making a big mistake."

The days went by and Steven's name wasn't mentioned in our house. Life fell back into it's usual routine, but I felt lost and empty. One morning I received a letter inviting me to go for an interview for the Head of English position, I didn't even feel like going I was so down. My daughters tried to show some enthusiasm and when the time came for me to go I started to feel a little bit more enthusiastic. I dressed carefully in my new grey suit and white blouse and arrived in good time. There were six of us sitting waiting, four women, and two men. I was the second to be called in, I didn't feel particularly nervous, and felt the interview went quite well. I was told that I would be informed whether I had been given the position or not in a few days' time. When I arrived home that night, my daughters had prepared tea, and they all asked me how the interview had gone. Jed stayed in his room, came down and ate his tea and then went out, he never even mentioned my interview. I felt very hurt and realised what a selfish young man he was becoming.

Three days later I received a letter telling me that I had been chosen. I was so excited and my daughters were over the moon, I didn't even bother to tell Jed. I was going to receive a much better salary but also more responsibility. Beverly Davies was stepping up a rung and I was pleased about that, she was a lovely person and she and I worked well together. I hadn't heard from either Steven or John and I had been so busy I hadn't had time to contact them, but I didn't have long to wait. As soon as Beverly told her dad about my promotion he got in touch. I came out of school one night and started to walk to the bus stop when I saw his car, he beckoned me to go over, I opened the car door. "Do get in," he said. "Hello, John," I replied as I climbed into the passenger seat, "it's good to see you." "Hello, Annie," he said, "I'm so sorry I haven't been in touch but I have been working away for a while starting up a new branch of the Bank and I have only just come back home." He started the car and said, "are you in a hurry to get home or can we go out somewhere?" "I must go home John," I replied, "my girls will wonder where I am." He drove me home and we sat outside my front door and chatted. "He said how pleased he was that I had been promoted and asked if I would like to go out one night?" "Yes, of course," I replied, "but I've a lot to do this week. Can we maybe make it Saturday evening?" "Yes, that's fine by me," said John, "I will pick you up at seven thirty and I will think of somewhere for us to go." He leaned over and kissed my cheek as I climbed out of the car and went indoors. "Who's car was that?" said Sally. I explained who it was. "Why didn't you invite him in?" said Angela. "Oh! I don't know," I replied, "I will bring him in to meet you some other time, and by the way I'm going out with him on Saturday night." "What about Steven?" said Sally. "What do you mean, what about Steven. Steven and me are just good friends so I can go out with whom I like," I answered.

Saturday soon came round and I found myself carefully deciding what to wear for my night out with John. I had a leisurely bath and Natalie curled my hair and did my make up. I chose a new dress I had bought recently and I hoped I looked nice. John arrived on time and I was soon in his car and we were away. "My you look lovely Annie," he said as we drove away. "Thank you," I said, "my daughter Natalie has helped me to get ready." "She must be doing well," he replied, and I thought about how hard she had worked and was now a qualified beautician. "I've booked for us to see the musical 'My Fair Lady' at the Alhambra," he said, "I hope that's alright with you and afterwards I have reserved a table at the Savoy." "Oh! John that sounds wonderful," I replied.

The evening went by like a dream and when it was time to go home I felt so happy. John drove carefully through the night and we were soon at my front door. "John, I can't begin to tell you how much I have enjoyed myself," I said. John leaned across and put his arm around my shoulder. "I'm so pleased Annie, I must say it's been a magical evening," and he leaned over and kissed me. I returned his kiss with a passion I had suppressed for so long. "You know I am in love with you Annie," said this lovely man as he released himself from our kiss. "I would love to think you might feel the same." "John," I replied, "I do care for you very deeply but I am not yet ready for a relationship." "I won't put any pressure on you Annie, but I can't help but love you," and he kissed me again. This time I felt a feeling inside me that was so unreal. I wanted this man so much but I knew I had to say 'Goodnight'. "Goodnight, my darling Annie," said John, "thank you for everything." He escorted me to my front door and he held me in his arms as we kissed goodnight. I went into the house and my head was in the clouds. The clock said two thirty and I was glad my family were in bed. I made myself a hot drink and climbed the stairs. Sleep evaded me as I thought about John and the lovely evening we had spent together. I could still feel his arms around me and, I knew I was falling deeply in love with this wonderful man.

Chapter 25

The next few weeks I was kept very busy, I didn't have time to dwell on my love life. I had meetings to attend as well as my teaching job. Joanne's graduation day was near and I had to take a few days leave to attend. Alison announced she was getting married and would be coming home to make all the arrangements. When the next school holiday arrived I was beginning to feel ready for a break. I had seen little of Steven, he was busy settling into his new home, and, although I had been there with him on a couple of occasions, I hadn't done much to help him. John knew of my situation at work and had kept a low profile. When I did see him we usually went for a quiet drink somewhere and I loved being in his company.

When Alison arrived home we talked non-stop and she was able to accompany me to Joanne's graduation. She had bought her own car so we travelled in style and it was nice not to have to catch the train. We spent an interesting four days in London. Here I was with my two elder daughters and I think I was the proudest mother in the room when Joanne's name was called and she walked on to the stage to receive her diploma. Joanne was able to return with us and when we arrived home it was good to have my entire family together under one roof. We never seemed to stop talking and, of course the main subject was Alison's wedding, she wanted to be married at our local church and all her sisters were to be bridesmaids. Joanne had to find out if she would be able to take time off, she was about to start work at the Children's Hospital in Bristol. Jed found the whole thing terribly boring and whenever we started on about the wedding he usually vanished to his friend's house, in fact he seemed to spend more time at Richards than he did at home.

Of course, my daughters had not missed the fact that Steven was not around so much and I had mentioned John's name a few times. "Tell me mum what's happened to Steven Bratley?" said Joanne one morning as we were finishing breakfast and I was about to leave for school. "You don't seem to see him now do you?" "Oh! I don't know love I've been too busy to see him," I replied, "Anyway I must go or I'll miss my bus." "I'll take you in the car," said Alison. "That's alright," I said, "I don't mind going on the bus, besides you're still in your dressing gown." So off I went and realised I had managed to get away without answering Joanne's question about Steven. That evening my daughters were going for the last fitting for their bridesmaid dresses, Alison's dress was completed. We all went round to the dressmakers, and as each of my girls paraded in front of me in their very pale blue dresses I thought how beautiful they all looked and a huge lump came into my throat. What would my Jed have thought, he had missed so much of their lives, and I had to catch my breath and wipe a tear from my eyes. "Don't be upset mum," said Alison, "this is supposed to be a happy time." "I'm sorry," I said, "but I can't help thinking what our lives would have been like if your dad had lived." She put her arm around my shoulder and whispered, "we all love you mum and I feel sure dad will be watching us from above." I squeezed her hand and thought what a wonderful family I had.

Joanne and Alison had to go back a few days later and all the arrangements had been made for the wedding, the only thing outstanding was asking Jed to give her away. "Just ask him outright," I said. "He's bound to refuse," said Alison. "We'll wait till he's had his tea tonight and then ask him," I replied. Sure enough Alison waited. When he had finished eating he jumped up from the table and said he had work to do and was going to his room. "Just one moment young man," I said, "Alison wants to talk to you." He turned round and looked at Alison. "What do you want me for?" he grunted, "I was wondering Jed if you would give me away at my wedding?" said Alison. "You must be joking," he replied, "no way," and he made to walk out of the room. "Hang on a minute Jed," I said, "I think you should listen to Alison." "But mother I don't even want to go to the wedding never mind act as the bride's father. Can't you ask somebody else?" he said. "I don't think you are being very fair to your sister," I answered. "What with you marrying that Steven Bratley and our Alison wanting me to give her away, I don't want to know," he snarled and slammed out of the back door. Alison jumped up to go after him. "Oh leave him be," I said, "he'll come round." "Yes but mother he needs taking in hand," said Alison, "You gave up your chance of a new life when you turned down Steven's proposal and you only did it for my selfish brother. Why do you let him get away with it?" I went over to where she was sitting and put my arms around her. "Look love," I said, "your brother is very young and has a lot to learn. He has been brought up in a family of women and has never known his dad. Let's just be gentle with him I am sure he will come round in a few days, leave it to me I will talk to him."

The big day soon arrived and I woke to a pale sun shining through my window. We spent a hectic morning getting ready and as I left for the church I looked at my daughters and couldn't quite believe they were all mine. I took my place in the church and waited for the bridal march to begin. I turned around and saw my Alison in her gown of gossamer silk holding the arm of my big stubborn son. What a picture they made with my four lovely daughters following behind in their beautiful dresses. I thought of my Jed and somehow I felt his presence and as Alison and David took their vows I knew he was watching over us.

During the evening's celebrations I chatted with all the guests. Our lovely friends and neighbours, but one person had not been well enough to attend and that was my dear friend Mary Doherty. She hadn't been well and her age was against her making the long journey across the Irish Sea. Oh! how I would have loved her to have been here with us. Steven looked nice and I was able to sit and have a chat with him. He told me how happy he was now he was settled in his new home and I promised I would go up there when I had the time. Harold Sutton came with his wife and two young children. He hadn't changed much and we laughed and talked about our school days.

As my newly married daughter drove off into the night everyone began to drift away. That night as I lay in my bed, sleep evaded me and I thought about the day's events and I remembered my own wedding and how different life was now. I could see my Grandma Pointer sitting there with her library books and her chocolate and I thought about the many times she had hit me. My poor mother working so hard and Alfie coming into her life and making things easier for her. My lovely grandma Clayton. My dad sitting in the old tin bath in front of the fire while mum scrubbed his back. Then I thought of my Jed and the tears were not far away. How could I marry anyone else when I still loved him so? I sobbed into my pillow and fell into a fitful sleep.

The next day we all seemed very subdued. I had a headache; Joanne was busy packing to go back to Bristol. Jed didn't show his face till nearly lunchtime and even he didn't seem very talkative. I busied myself doing jobs that didn't really need doing and it was quite a relief to get back to work on Monday morning. Beverley came into my office, she couldn't stop talking about the wedding, and she brought me a note from her dad. I slit open the envelope and John was asking me to go out with him, Thursday evening, 8 o'clock he would pick me up. I found myself looking forward to his arrival and when his car pulled up at the front of my house I was ready and waiting. I jumped in the car and said, "Hello John it's lovely to see you again." "Hello Annie," he replied, "it's lovely to see you too. Why have we left it so long?" We drove in silence for a while. "I thought we'd go and have a bite to eat," John said, and he carefully parked the car outside a restaurant unfamiliar to me. We were shown to our table and the waitress appeared. After we had ordered John turned to me and said, "Annie I have missed you so much. I have tried to keep away from you, but I so love having you near to me." "I have missed you too John, but I have been so busy what with the wedding and everything," I replied. He reached for my hand and my heart did a leap. He looked so handsome and I felt happy to be with this attractive man. Our food arrived and we ate in silence, after we had eaten our light-hearted conversation flowed and it was good to be so at ease. John drove me home and I invited him into my house. Jed was in his room and Sally and Angela were out. Natalie was busy preparing her supper and was about to go to bed. John followed me into the kitchen; I introduced him to my daughter. I think she felt a bit embarrassed as she was in her dressing gown. John shook her hand and said how pleased he was to meet her and she disappeared off to bed. "Ask Jed to turn his music down," I said to her. Off she went upstairs and I could hear her talking to Jed. He flew downstairs and took one look at John, "Who are you and what are you doing here?" he snapped, his face was like thunder." That's enough of that kind of talk," I said as I went over to him. "It's alright Annie," said John, "I understand, I will be on my way." "No, don't go," I replied, "Jed has no right to speak to you like that, he must apologise." "No, I will not," said Jed and banged back upstairs. "I'm so sorry John," I said, "I had no idea this was going to happen." "Don't worry," replied John, "I'd better go anyway," and he went to the door. I stood beside him and said, "Goodnight," and he put his arms around me and held me close. "Goodnight my darling," he said, and he was gone.

I charged back up the stairs and opened Jed's bedroom door. "How dare you speak to my friend like that?" I said, "and turn that music off." "I don't like him," he retorted. "You don't even know him," I replied. "No, and I don't want to know him anyway," he said. Natalie came into the room. "What's going on?" she said. "Nothing that concerns you," said Jed, "and get out of my room." Natalie turned to me, "What's wrong mum?" she said. "Oh! It's only your big brother being rude to my friend," I replied. "I was not rude, I just don't like him that's all," said Jed, "and you keep out of it." "That's enough now Jed," I said. "No it's not, I don't like you going out with that man," he replied, and I could see he was very upset. "Go back to your room Natalie, I can sort it out," I said. "But I don't like leaving you mum," she replied. "Don't worry love I'll be alright." She was about to say something to Jed but thought better of it and as she left the room she gave me a kiss and said goodnight.

I turned to my son and looked at his big sorrowful eyes. He turned his head and I said, "What's wrong Jed. Why are you behaving like a spoilt schoolboy? Are you never going to like my friends?" A look of contrition was on his face. "I'm sorry mum but I don't like you having someone in dad's place," he whispered. "I've told you before Jed no one will ever replace your dad in my heart, but I do like to go out with John he is a very nice person," I replied. He looked so vulnerable sitting there on the edge of his bed. I went and sat beside him and I reached for his hand. "Come on sweetheart," I said, "please try and accept John for my sake." "Yes, but mum what if he wants you to marry you, then what's going to happen to us?" he muttered. "Don't even think about it," I replied, "we will face up to that if ever the time comes. Come on now let's have you settling down. You've got to be up early in the morning." I felt I was talking to a small five year old instead of my big hunk of a son, Jed. I kissed his cheek and I realised there were tears in his eyes, I felt so sorry for him, not having a father had made a big impact on his life. As I went into my bedroom I heard Sally and Angela arriving home. I quickly turned off my light. I did not want to have any questions from them tonight.

The next few weeks passed without incident and I began to relax and forget about what had happened between Jed and John and I had made up my mind to stop seeing either John or Steven. I thought it was better to let things calm down and when the next school holiday approached I decided to take myself off to see Mary in Ireland. I knew I always felt better when I had been to see her and also I was worried about how she was keeping. I soon arranged my visit and arrived at Mary's cottage with so much hope in my heart. She greeted me with open arms. This little frail old lady who had helped me so much over the years. "Hello my dear, it's lovely to see you," her voice lilted. "Hello, Mary," I answered, "it's so good to be here," and I held her in my arms. She looked very worn and tired. "Come on," she said, "let me put the kettle on." I sat in the nearest chair while Mary came back with the tray and placed it by her side. She busied herself pouring the tea and I noticed she had made some little cakes for my coming. "How are you Mary?" I asked. "Oh! I'm fine," she replied, "but I must hear all your news." We talked well into the night and I filled her in with the things that had been happening in my family. I told her all about the wedding and she listened avidly. She asked about my girls and I told her how they were getting on. She then asked about Jed and I skirted round the truth and just told her about his work. "There's something you're not telling me, isn't there?" she said. This canny little old lady didn't miss a thing. "It's nothing really," I replied. "Yes, but what about Steven?" she asked. I couldn't believe how she remembered everything. So I filled her in with what was happening in my love life. "You must not give in to this young scoundrel," she said, "he has no right to stop you going out with who ever you like. You deserve some happiness in your life and you shouldn't take any notice of what Jed thinks." I tried to explain to her how I felt. I told her I wanted Jed to be in favour of any relationship I had. "But he's only thinking of himself," she said. "Well I'm going to wait until he's older and he may have a better understanding," I replied. "Your life is passing by and you deserve to have someone at your side to love you and be with you, and to make up for all sadness you have endured," she said. I got up and sat on the arm of her chair and put my arms around her frail shoulders and gave her a hug. "Well we will see how things go when I get home," I said, "come on now let's go to bed."

I spent an idyllic ten days at Mary's home. We had little walks on the beach and we visited her local church and met some of her friends who remembered me from when I visited before. I felt so relaxed and when it was time to leave I had so much peace in my heart and as I said, 'Goodbye' to my lovely friend I felt so grateful to have this wonderful lady in my life.

On my return home, Steven met me at the station and he drove me home. I looked at this dear man who had always been there for me and I wanted to tell him just how much he meant to me, but the words would not come out. I invited him in for a cup of tea and we sat and talked. He asked me about my holiday and he filled me in with all the local news. My dear, dear Steven, how could I have turned down his proposal? When it was time for him to go I linked my arm through his and walked to the door. "Before you go Steven," I said, "I have something I want to say to you." He turned his head and looked down at me. "What is it Annie?" he said, "nothing wrong I hope." "No, my darling," I answered, "everything is fine. I just wanted to say if you still want us to be married, I would like to accept your proposal." He looked at me with disbelief. "Oh! Annie!" he said, "of course I still want us to be married, but are you sure?" "Yes, I have never been so sure of anything in my life," I replied, and I lifted my head for his kiss. He wrapped me in his arms and tears of joy fell down our faces as he kissed me with a passion I hadn't felt for such a long time.

I soon unpacked and waited for my family to arrive home. I was so very happy and knew my decision had been the right one. It had taken a visit to my friend to make me realise how much I loved Steven. I thought about John and the lovely times we had spent together, but I was certain in my heart my future was with Steven. How strange, it had taken me all this time to realise how much I loved him. My girls arrived home from work and it was great to see them again. After they had eaten we sat and chatted. They wanted to hear all about my holiday and how Mary was. I filled them in with all my news and listened to their stories. Sally was going to become engaged to her Paul, Angela had a new boyfriend, Andy, who I had yet to meet and Natalie had been promoted at work and was now in charge at the beauty salon. When we had finished chatting I went to fetch the bottle of sherry we kept in the top cupboard. I picked up four glasses and proceeded to fill them. "What's going on Mum?" said Sally as I handed round the sherry. "Sit down all of you," I said, "I have something to tell you." "Nothing wrong is there Mum?" said Natalie. "No, my darlings," I replied. "What I want to tell you is that I have agreed to marry Steven, and I would like us to drink a toast to let you know how happy I am." My daughters' faces were a picture. Angela was the first to speak. "This is lovely news Mum," and she put her arms around me followed by Sally and Natalie. We drank our sherry and then Jed walked in. "Hello Mum," he said, "it's good to have you home," and he came and gave me a kiss. "It's good to be home son," I replied. "Why are you all drinking sherry," he said, "is there something to celebrate?" "Yes there is," said Sally, "mum is going to marry Steven." I watched his face and he turned to me and said, "Ok! Mum if that is what you want, but I can't say I like the idea." I went over to him and linked my arm through his. "Thank you Jed," I said "I know Steven will make me happy and I am sure you will be happy too," and poured him a glass of sherry.

I knew the next thing I had to do was let John know of my decision to marry Steven. I rang him and asked him if we could meet. "Yes, of course," he said and arranged to pick me up from school the following night. I climbed into his car and we drove out into the countryside. We stopped and I told John I had something to tell him. "What is it Annie?" he said, "you are alright, not ill or anything." "No I'm alright, but I wanted you to know I am going to be married." I explained to him about my feelings for Steven and thanked him for the lovely times we had spent together. "Thank you for telling me Annie," he said, "I couldn't help falling in love with you but somehow I knew you didn't feel for me in the same way," and he reached out and held my hand. "I'm sorry John, I have valued our friendship and I hope you will still keep in touch," I said. He drove me back home and I said goodbye to a very wonderful friend.

Steven and I were married in a very quiet ceremony and, as we took our vows, I realised how very much I loved this lovely man standing at the side of me. We had a small reception, and both our families were with us. Steven's parents were there looking very proud. His dad was now in a wheelchair, as he couldn't walk very far. My big surly son was on his best behaviour and even he seemed to be happy for me. But the one special person I wanted to be there with us was missing and that was Mary. She had written and given us her blessing, but sadly couldn't make it.

I had spent the last few weeks moving my belongings to Steven's house. This lovely big house standing at the top of the hill overlooking the countryside. So much different from my little terrace house with the view of the pit and the dirt and smoke all around. Steven had gone to the trouble to have the place decorated for me and had employed a professional decorator. Whilst I was up at the house sorting out my possessions, I could hear this canny fellow, who originated from Northumberland, singing the day away whilst he was busy with his paint and brushes. Every room looked perfect.

It had been decided that my family would stay on in Colliery Terrace. The National Coal Board had agreed to let my family stay in the house, and my daughters assured me they would keep an eye on Jed. I did suggest he could come and live with Steven and me, but he didn't want to. I was beginning to think my son was starting to grow up after all.

We set off for our honeymoon destination. Steven had booked a few days in a lovely hotel overlooking the sea at a town on the east coast. I felt so happy as I unpacked my case, and as I looked at my lovely husband my heart was bursting. "Hello there Mrs Bratley," said Steven and he came across the room and put his arms around me. "Hello there my darling Steven," I replied, and we held each other tight. Steven whispered in my ear "I love you so very much my Annie, thank you for making me the happiest man in the world." That night, as we made love our feelings, which had been suppressed for so many years could now be released and I knew deep in my heart I loved Steven so very much. I asked myself why had I waited so long. We spent an idyllic four days together and when we returned home I soon settled in Steven's lovely house and we both returned to work and our lives now had a new meaning.

It seemed strange living in such a big house and I revelled in the luxury of it all. I saw my children every day and they seemed to be coping well without me. It seemed strange when I went back to 99 Colliery Terrace. I had lived there for so long and part of me would always be there, but being with Steven was an absolute joy.

Jed had finished his training and was now working underground. This was the only thing that marred my happiness, but I had to let him follow what he wanted to do, so I just had to stand by and let him get on with it. Sally and Paul were arranging their wedding and were going to buy their own house. Paul worked for a firm of lawyers and was doing quite well in his chosen profession, he was a likeable person and seemed to idolise Sally. Angela seemed to be quite happy with her Andy. He was a plumber and could turn his had to most household jobs. Natalie was always inviting me to go in for a facial and massage, but I never seemed to have the time. I heard regularly from Alison and Joanne. Alison was managing to hold down her teaching job and still find time for her husband David, while Joanne had settled well into her job at the children's hospital and was going to become engaged to one of the doctors she worked with. I hadn't yet met him but knew his name was Simon. As for my life, I couldn't believe how happy I was. I would never forget my Jed, after all he had given me my lovely family, but Steven brought me so much happiness and our life together was like a dream.

Chapter 26

One morning, I was summoned to the head teacher's office. I was terribly busy and wondered why she needed to see me. "Do sit down," she said to me as I went in. "You will probably wonder why I have sent for you," she said. "There's nothing wrong I hope?" I replied. "No everything is fine, I want to congratulate you on the work you have been doing in your department, you have done a fine job." "Thank you so much," I replied. "What I want to tell you," she continued," is that I am retiring at the end of the term and I wondered if you are interested in applying for the job as Head of the School?" I looked at her in amazement. "I think you would make a very good Head Teacher, and with your permission I would like to put your name forward for consideration." My throat was dry as I tried to answer her. "Well yes, of course", I managed to stammer, "I would be greatly honoured to become Head of the School if you think I'm up to it." "Well leave it to me," she replied, "I will inform the School Governors of your interest." I left the room in a daze and couldn't wait to tell Steven. He was so happy for me and when the day came for my interview I felt very moved to think I had a chance to become Head Teacher of a school, which had played such a big part in my life. The interview went well and I was told I would be hearing in the next few weeks whether I had been successful or not. I knew there were quite a few people had applied for the position so I dare not raise my hopes too much.

Exactly two weeks after my interview I received a letter telling me I had been successful, and I would be taking up the position as Head of Sotherly High School when the new term started in September. I was so elated and couldn't believe how happy I was. Steven wrapped his arms around me and said we must go and tell all the gang at No.99. They were all so pleased and even Jed put his arm around my shoulders and said, "Good for you Mum, I told you could do it."

I took up my position straight after the summer holidays. I knew this was a big undertaking and I had so much to give. Beverley Davis was promoted to my old position, as Head of English and I knew she would make a good job of it. My life fell into a lovely routine and as the weeks went on I felt so happy and content.

One morning, I had just returned to my office after taking morning assembly when there was a knock at the door. "Come in," I called. Standing there was one of the school prefects. "What's wrong Isobel?" I said. "There's a man to see you Miss in the school corridor," she replied. "Who is it?" I questioned, "why don't you bring him in?" "He wouldn't come in Miss and I don't know who it is," she answered, "he just said it was urgent." "Alright, I'll be right along," I said, and I followed her out of the door to see who was there. Standing there, twisting his cap in his hands was Andy Purshouse. I hadn't seen him for quite a while, but I still knew him. "What's wrong Andy?" I said. "Best come quickly Annie," he said, "Somats happened at pit and your Jeds down there." I felt my blood run cold as I fetched my coat and ran as fast as I could. I didn't even tell anyone where I was going. Outside Andy was waiting for me in an old van. We didn't speak as he quickly drove through the traffic. When we reached the pit, I jumped out and ran to where I could see the men gathering on the pit top. I could hear the clanging of the fire engines in the distance. "What's wrong?" I said to the nearest man I came to. "Been an explosion Mrs," he said. I felt my stomach lurch as I went near to the pithead. "Best stay back luv," said one man, "don't need women getting in the way." I walked back and saw some more women arriving in the pit yard. "Clear the way," said one fireman as he carried his fire fighting equipment and entered the pit cage. He was joined by some more fire fighters as I heard the clanging of the ambulances in the distance. I went to stand with the other women, some of whom I recognised. "What's happening?" said Linda Purshouse. I knew both her sons worked in the pit. "I don't know," I answered, "somebody said there'd been an explosion" "Oh my God," said Linda, "both our Barry and Bill are on this shift." "Is your Jed down there?" she said. "Yes, he is," I said, and I could feel my whole body shaking with fear. Linda came and stood beside me. Neither of us spoke. Some of the women began to cry, but I just felt numb. "Please God, let him be alright," I said to myself. We huddled together in the cold and as I looked around me I realised nothing had changed. After all these years the dirty depressing pit had not altered in anyway. I stood as I had stood before, waiting for news of my son, just like it had been for my dear husband, my father, grandfather, and father-in-law before him. This relentless pit was never going to change and while ever the poor men toiled underground their lives would always be in peril. I shivered and pulled my coat tighter around me and stared blankly ahead. Everything seemed deathly quiet; the only sounds were the clanging of the ambulances as they raced to the scene. Two fire engines stood in front of us, but the firemen were underground. I just wish someone would bring us some news, I thought to myself as more women joined our group. An hour must have passed before we saw the wheels turning at the top of the pit shaft. We all pushed forward but the waiting officials held us back. One woman called, "What's happening, please let us know?" and we all echoed her request. When the pit cage reached the top there was a hive of activity as the safety barriers clanged across. I strained my neck to try and see, but someone blocked my view. Then I saw the stretchers as the men were carried into the waiting ambulances. The bells began to clang and they were off to the hospital in no time. Still no one talked to us and one young woman became quite hysterical. I looked at her heavily pregnant body and my memories came back. Poor girl what was to become of her?

After what seemed like an eternity one man came forward to talk to us. "I'm sorry ladies," he said, "but there has been an explosion underground. As yet, we don't know what's caused it, but I'm afraid a lot of men have been killed, some badly injured and most of the injuries are burns." I felt my legs buckle under me and if it had not been for Linda Purshouse I would have keeled over. She held on tight to my arm and I reached out to the nearby railings for support. "Are you alright Annie?" she asked, "yes, I just felt faint that's all, I am sorry." "There's nothing to be sorry about," she answered, "I know what you've been through." "Yes, but you've got two lads down there, you don't need me as a burden," I replied. "What will be, will be," she said, "it's all in God's hands now."

The time dragged slowly by and the ambulances ferried the men to the hospital. Eventually, the Pit Manager came to talk to us, "I'm sorry I can't help you ladies, but until we can sort out who is who I think it would be better if you all returned to your homes, and as soon as we know what's happening we will send someone to see you. There's not much you can do waiting here and you are only getting more distressed." Slowly we all dispersed and I found myself heading to Colliery Terrace. I let myself in and looked at the time, it was three o'clock. Automatically, I put the kettle on and sat on the kitchen chair, I sipped my tea and prayed for my son. I held my head in my hands and felt so numb. How long I was sitting there I do not know when I heard heavy banging at the back door. I jumped up and opened it. Standing there was Andy Purshouse. "Come in Andy," I said. He took off his cap and came into the kitchen. "I'm sorry Annie," he said, "it's bad news, your Jed has been badly hurt and is in a serious condition." "Oh no!" I answered, "where is he, take me to him?" I pulled on my coat and rushed out of the door. I jumped into Andy's battered old van and we drove to the hospital.

When we arrived I was ushered into the waiting room. All the women were gathered there and some kind person had brought us all a cup of tea. I picked out Linda Purshouse and went to sit beside her. She reached out for my hand and said, "try not to worry Annie, I'm sure he'll be alright." Oh! if only I could believe her, I thought. "What about your boys Linda?" I said. "No news yet I'm afraid," she answered, and we sat there waiting. No one spoke, and after what seemed an age, a tall man in a white coat entered the room. He cleared his throat and began to speak "Our sympathies are with you all," he said, "we have now managed to assess the severity of the injuries to your men folk. There have been two fatalities and some very serious injuries." I felt myself reach out for Linda Purshouse; she held my hand as this man carried on talking. "I'm sorry to say both Jack Balding and Ernest Merryweather were killed outright, both their wives have been told and are being taken care of. Three men have received very serious burns and are receiving our best attention; their names are as follows, Sam Cookson, Owen Brownlow, and Jed Harper. I felt myself keel over and Linda held me. A nurse came over to where I was sitting and I was taken to another room. When I came round, the other two women were in the room with me. Jean Cookson and Brenda Brownlow were crying hysterically and were being held by one of the nurses. "Is there anyone we can get to be with you?" she said. I thought for a moment and asked her to bring my daughters here. I told her where to reach them and she passed the information onto one of the junior nurses. "Can I see my Jed?" I asked. "Not for a while the doctors are still with him," she answered. "What are his chances?" I asked. "I'm sorry I don't know, but as soon as there is any news you will be informed," she answered. Suddenly I looked up and Sally was coming across the room, I stood up as she reached me and she put her arms around me and we cried together. Five minutes later Angela and Natalie came in, I could see Natalie had been crying and Angela gave me a hug. "Oh! Mum," she said, "whatever has happened?" We all sat together and we waited for the news of our Jed.

Jean Cookson was first to be called and she was taken through by one of the nurses. The poor woman could hardly walk and she was held tightly as she struggled along. We were brought some hot sweet tea and we waited and waited. I looked around the room and realised I had been here before, waiting with Mary for news of my Jed. My memories came back and I was pleased to have my daughters here with me. Brenda Brownlow was taken through to see her son and we were left waiting. After what seemed an eternity, it was our turn. "I'm sorry," said the man in the white coat, "but only one person is allowed to be with Mr Harper," as we all got up to go through. "Please let my daughters come with me," I managed to say. "Well perhaps one of them," he replied. Sally took my arm and Angela and Natalie went back to their seats. We walked along the now familiar corridors. The man in the white coat turned and said "I'm Peter Osborne, your son's doctor," and he held my hand. "I must warn you that your son has been very badly injured. He has sixty percent burns to his body and I'm afraid his chances of surviving are not good." "You can see him for a few minutes and then you must leave." We entered Jed's room, a shaft of light shone through the high window. As we approached the bed, Peter Osborne quietly left us. Lying there swathed in bandages was my lovely son, Jed, his head, and shoulders were wrapped and we could only pick out part of his face. His black hair was shorn and burnt and his body was lifeless. Sally clung to me as we held each other up. A tall bright nurse came hustling into the room. She came to where we were standing. "Are you alright?" she said in a low voice. "Yes, thank you," I managed to whisper. She said her name was Bernice Kelly and she would be looking after Jed. As I stood and looked at my son, my heart went out to him. This can't be happening again I thought to myself, but here I was in this old dreaded place of a hospital, watching over one of my beloved family who had succumbed to the terrors of the cruel underground workings that we called coal pits.

We were gently ushered out of the room and told we would be kept informed of any change in his condition and we went back to collect Angela and Natalie from the waiting room. As we reached the main doors, I saw my Steven coming towards us. He came to me and put his arms around me. "Oh! my darling," he said, "whatever has happened?" and I sobbed in his arms. We all climbed into his car and he carefully drove us home. We were all distraught and my three lovely daughters were so bewildered. Steven was a rock; he took over and sorted us all out. "You must all stay here tonight," he said to my girls, your mother will need you," and I was so grateful for his help. The next day he informed the school and the Deputy Head, Muriel Cooper said to take as much time away as needed. My daughters stayed with me, but there was no news from the hospital, I needed to be there and Steven took us all back. We approached the building with great trepidation, and went into the waiting room; Steven went to ask about Jed. "There is no change in his condition," he said when he came back to us. "I wonder if I can see him Steven?" I said. "You can but ask," he answered. I went over to the young lady receptionist and she said she would make enquiries, and I waited. "Yes, you can go in and see him now," she said, "but Dr Osborne says you can only stay ten minutes." We all set off to walk down the corridor, but were called back by the receptionist. "Only two of you can go in," she said. We stopped and agreed that Angela would accompany me. We quietly opened the door and entered Jed's room. The nurse was sitting holding Jed's hand, she looked up as we entered, "Hello," she said, and I could hear the hint of an Irish lilt in her voice. "How is he?" I whispered. "Oh, I think he seems better this morning," she said. I moved over to my son's bedside and looked down at his swathed face. "Yes I think he does look more rested than he did last night," I said, as the nurse left the room. Angela leaned over her brother, she whispered to him, "Please Jed come back to us soon," as tears rolled down her cheeks, "I will go Mum and let you have him to yourself" she sobbed. "Send Natalie in will you Angela, I think she wants to see her brother," and she quietly left the room. I sat at Jed's bedside and held his hand, "Please Jed don't leave us," I whispered, "we all need you here," and I felt sure he could hear me. Natalie came into the room, she walked over to Jed and looked down at him. "Oh! mum what's going to happen to him?" she said and turned her head away. "I don't know sweetheart, all we can do is pray," I answered. Nurse Kelly entered the room. "I'm afraid you must go now," she said. "But we don't seem to have been here very long," I said. "It's been a full fifteen minutes," she replied, "but please come back tomorrow, I am sure you will be able to stop longer then. In the meantime I will take care of him." I thanked her and left the room. My tired and weary body felt numb with apprehension. I don't think I can get through this, I thought to myself, but I knew my girls needed me. This was all new to them and I had to be strong for their sakes. Steven took us home and we tried to bring some normality back into our lives. My daughters returned to their jobs and Steven had to go to work and I was left on my own. I went into school and saw Muriel Cooper. She was so kind to me and we sat and discussed what was happening in the school and she told me not to worry she would take over. I came out of school and caught the bus to the hospital. I was told I could go in and see Jed, but his condition hadn't changed. As I approached his room I could hear a soft singing voice with an Irish lilt. I opened the door and the little nurse was sitting there humming softly to my son. "Good morning," she said, as she turned round and saw me. "How is he?" I queried. "Pretty much the same," she answered, "but I feel sure he will pull through." I wish I felt as optimistic, I thought. She got up from her chair. "Would you like a cup of tea?" she asked. "Yes please that would be nice," I answered, and off she went. I sat in her vacated chair and looked at my son as I took hold of his hand. "Good morning my darling," I said very bravely, "how are you today?" and squeezed his hand. There was no response as I gazed at his battered body. Bernice Kelly brought me my tea and left me with Jed. I was able to stay with him for over an hour and as I was about to leave Dr Osborne came into the room. He came and stood beside me and shook my hand. "How is he doctor?" I asked. "Well! he is no better, but he is still with us and that means a great deal. I didn't expect him to last through the first night," he answered, "but I will not raise your hopes until we see how the next few days go, but Mr Harper is a strong young man and he certainly has youth on his side." I thanked him for his kindness and caught the bus home. As I arrived home there was a strange car parked on our drive. I wonder who this can be, I thought to myself. As I opened the door I heard voices. I rushed through to the kitchen and who should greet me but Alison and her husband. They were sitting drinking coffee and Alison jumped up and came towards me. We clung together and I said, "How long have you been here? Oh! what a lovely surprise." "We've just arrived mum," said Alison as David gave me a hug. "It's so good to see you," I answered, "I've just come from the hospital." "How is he mum?" said Alison. "Just the same I'm afraid. The doctor doesn't hold out much hope for him," I answered. But it was so good having my eldest daughter home. "Do you think we could go to see him?" she said. "I would think so," I answered, "but don't go just yet. Tell me all your news and I will prepare some food and we will all return to the hospital." "I will do the food mother," said Alison, "you sit down, you look all in." She quickly prepared some sandwiches and as we ate we never stopped talking. This was the first proper food I had eaten since the accident and I was enjoying the sandwiches she had prepared. "These are good Alison," I remarked. "Yes, you look as if you need looking after," she replied. "But Steven takes good care of me and so do your sisters," I answered. "I know they do," she said, "but I just need an excuse to mother you. How are they all anyway?" "Alright I think," I answered, "but terribly upset as you can well imagine." When we had finished eating Alison suggested her and David would go to the hospital on their own. "You stay at home and relax mum," she said, "it's only upsetting for you to be there." "Yes but I want to be with him," I replied. "Ok! then," she said, "come on," and we climbed into David's car and drove to the hospital. We had to wait for nearly an hour before we were allowed to go in and see him. Apparently there was a specialist examining Jed from the burns unit. When we did get in to see him it was the first time they allowed three of us to go in together. Alison approached his bed and I watched her gently lean over her brother. Her face turned deathly white and I thought she was going to keel over. David was soon at her side and he sat her down in the nearest chair. "Are you alright darling?" he said and I passed her a drink of water. "Yes' I'm alright," she replied, "just felt a bit dizzy." I put my arm around her shoulders. "Do you want to go home?" I asked. "No mum, I'm alright just give me a minute to come to," she answered. I looked at Jed and he didn't look any different. I reached for his hand and said, "Jed, Alison and David are here to see you, please wake up." But it was to no avail. The door opened and Nurse Kelly bustled in with a tray and a pot of tea and cups. "Thank you, so much," I said, "we really need this," and I introduced her to my daughter and her husband. "How is he today?" she asked, "I have only just come on duty." "Still the same," I replied. "But I believe Mr Foster has been to see him," she said. "Well I know someone has been to see him but I don't know who it was," I answered. "I'll go and find out what's happening," she said, and left the room. "Mum, doesn't she remind you of Mary," said Alison, "not in her looks but in her mannerisms and the way she speaks." "Yes, she does," I replied, "and she seems just as loving and kind as Mary." Ten minutes later she was back. "Is there any news?" I asked with my heart racing. "There's not much I can find out," she replied, "only that Mr Foster is assessing the possibility of doing skin grafts, but I don't think anything has been decided yet." I thanked her from the bottom of my heart and we said our goodbyes to Jed and left the hospital. Alison was in tears all the way home and when we arrived Steven was waiting for us. "How is he?" he questioned as he put his arms round Alison and me. I filled him in with the news from the hospital and Alison said they would have to leave soon. "But can't you stay the night?" asked Steven. "We've got to get back," replied David, "we both have to work tomorrow." But what about phoning in and explaining why you are here," I said. "Yes, Alison doesn't look at all well," said Steven. "It would be lovely if you could stay," I added. "What do you think David?" said Alison. "We could try," he answered. "Help yourself to the phone," said Steven. David managed to ring his boss and was told not to rush back. He then rang Alison's head teacher and said much the same thing. So I quickly made up the bed and we ate the food Steven had prepared for us and settled down for a quiet evening. Steven insisted on washing up and when he came to join us, David suddenly stood up. "Annie, Steven," he said, "we have something to tell you, Alison is going to have a baby and we are so excited." I jumped up from my chair and went over to my daughter. "Oh! my darling this is lovely news," I said, "I am so pleased for you." "Yes, mum we are so happy," she replied. "When is the baby due?" I asked. "Well the date I have been given is November 8th so I have about six months to go," she replied, "we haven't told any one yet till we were certain everything was alright." I was so happy for them but yet so upset that this good news was over shadowed by the tragedy in our lives.

Alison and David went to see Jed after breakfast next morning and stayed and had some lunch, then started their journey home. I was sorry to see them go but it had done me good to have them here. My other three daughters had been over and spent the evening with us and were so pleased with the news of the baby. The following day I went into school, there was so much to sort out but Muriel Cooper was doing a good job and I knew I could rely on her. The next two weeks I nearly lived at the hospital. I wanted to be near my son and, although he didn't know I was there I felt so much better for being with him. I had spoken to Dr Osborne and he had explained to me that skin grafts couldn't be performed until Jed was over the shock of the accident. All they could do for the time being was keep him sedated. Steven was a tower of strength and, when he wasn't at work he spent time with me at the hospital.

I sat and talked endlessly to Jed, it was always a one-way conversation, but I didn't mind I just felt he could hear me. One morning I arrived at the hospital and had to wait whilst the nurses changed his dressings. I was just about to get up from my chair in the waiting room when I heard a familiar voice. I went to the door and looked down the corridor. Coming towards me, assisted by one of the nurses, was my lovely dear friend, Mary Doherty. I ran towards her with tears rolling down my face, I reached out and clung to her. "Mary, oh! Mary what are you doing here?" I cried. She held me in her arms and we both cried together. "I had to come," she answered, "I couldn't let you go through this on your own." I looked at her dear kind face, she looked old and so tired but her eyes still twinkled and I was so pleased to see her. I took her arm as we walked towards Jed's room. I sat her down and knelt at her side. "Mary you will never know what this means to me," I said. She stroked my head and there we stayed till the door opened and in walked Nurse Kelly with the now familiar tray of tea. "Come on now you two," she said, "who's going to be mother?" I realised

I hadn't even looked at Jed, but when I did I felt much happier about him, he seemed to look better, or was that just my imagination?

I introduced Bernice Kelly to Mary and they shook hands and chatted away in their lovely Irish brogue. Mary recalled the days when she worked at this hospital and they discussed how nursing techniques had changed over the years. They talked of their homes in Ireland and it was lovely to hear their chatter. I looked at Jed and he seemed to have a much better look about him. His bandages had been removed and, although his head and face were still scarred, he seemed to be improving.

Bernice excused herself and Mary came to sit with me. "Seems a nice young lady she does," said Mary. "Yes she has taken good care of Jed," I answered. "I think he looks better," I said. She held Jed's hand and leaned over to look closely at him, and said, "but until he comes out of his coma we will not know just what the future holds for him."

We sat together with my son. We didn't need to talk and when it was time to go, Steven was waiting for us in the car park. "Mary this is Steven, my husband," I said as we sat in the car. "I've already met him," she replied. "What?" I queried, "You two have already met." "Well who do you think arranged all this, and who do you think met me off the boat?" Mary smiled. "Oh! Steven why didn't you tell me?" I asked. "I wanted it to be a surprise," he said. "Oh" my darling how can I ever thank you?" I said and reached over and held him close.

Mary stayed with us for the next two weeks and each day she accompanied me to the hospital. I swear I saw an improvement in Jed, but no one at the hospital gave me any reason to hope. Just having Mary with me helped me to feel better and we spent endless hours reminiscing about the old times. Yes, we had come through a lot together. When it was time for her to go, we both went to see her off. As we said our 'Good byes' I couldn't thank her enough for being with me when I needed her most. It must have been a big upheaval for this lovely old lady to travel all this way to be with me when she wasn't in the best of health.

Chapter 27

The enquiry into the disaster had been completed and we were informed that a spark had ignited gasses in the pit and the fire had spread very quickly. The poor men working in the vicinity had not stood a chance, but this was no consolation to the women left behind. Talks of compensation were being put forward, but this had no meaning for me. I just wanted my son to come back to me, no matter what condition he was in. I had now been away from my job for six weeks and I knew it was time for me to return, but I didn't want to leave my son. He was still deeply unconscious and was only clinging to life, but I lived in hope that I would arrive at his bedside one day and he would open his eyes and say 'Hello mum.' The doctors didn't hold out much hope and, each day I would sit and hold his hand and will him to live. I felt I couldn't go on with life if I lost him. One day Steven suggested I try going back to work, he could see how the strain was affecting me. I didn't feel as though I could go back but agreed to give it a try.

Everyone seemed pleased to see me on my return. Even the children seemed concerned about me, and, I must admit it was nice to be back in my old familiar surroundings. It still felt strange to be Head of this school, and I was grateful to have been given this opportunity to do the work I loved. As I left school each day I went straight to the hospital and stayed with Jed as long as the doctors would allow me to. Nothing had changed, and each day I wondered how much longer he had to live. One morning during assembly, I was talking to the pupils when my school secretary beckoned me to my office. I quickly went over to see what she wanted me for and was informed there was an urgent telephone call for me. I left the assembly in charge of Muriel Cooper and quickly picked up the phone. "Mrs Bratley," the voice said. "Yes that's right, I'm Mrs Bratley," I answered, "what do you want?" "It's the hospital calling," came the answer, "Jenny Cummings, one of the nurses on your son's ward. Can you come at once, there has been a change in your son's condition. He has shown a sign of improvement." "Oh! my goodness, is he alright?" I babbled. "Yes he's fine but can you come?" she said. "I'm on my way," I answered, and I was shaking like a leaf as Elaine Thompson, one of the teachers, said she would run me there. As she dropped me off at the hospital, she said, "Will you be alright?" "Yes, I'm fine," I answered, and ran into the corridor, which led to Jed's room. I quickly knocked on the door and went in, Bernice Kelly and another nurse were in the room and it was obvious they were changing his dressings. "Oh! do come in Mrs Bratley," said Bernice, "I am so glad you are here. Jed has shown a sign of movement." I moved over to the side of his bed. I could see the damage done to his skin, but I didn't care. I could see my son looked better than he had done for weeks and I wanted to hug him. "Tell me what's happened?" I said. "Just let us finish his dressings and then we can talk," replied Bernice Kelly. I sat in the corner and waited. When they had finished I looked at Jed and he seemed to be breathing easier. "Let us go to the nurses room and we will talk there," said the other nurse. We went along the corridor and into the nurse's room. "Sit down and we will have some tea," she said. I gratefully sat in the nearest chair and she made a pot of tea and came and sat beside me. "I am Sharon Skelton," she said, "I am staff nurse to your son. We haven't met before as I have only just started working here." She poured the tea and passed me a cup. "Oh! please don't keep me waiting any longer," I begged. "Well this morning, as I took over from night nurse, she reported having seen your son's eyes flickering, so I sat with him to see if I noticed anything. Shortly before we rang you I saw a definite movement and reported it to the doctor on the ward. He told me to let you know and to get you here. Now you have to be warned there may be no significance in this but we have to be hopeful." "But I must go to him," I said, "what if he is coming out of his coma?" "Its quite all right Nurse Kelly is with him. Just drink your tea and we will go straight back to his room," she answered. I gulped down the hot sweet liquid as quickly as I could and we went back to Jed's room.

Bernice Kelly was sitting with him. "Any change?" said Sharon Skelton. "No, nothing at all," she replied. "Well you can go now," said Sharon, and Bernice left the room. "I suggest you sit here with him and if you see any change in him just press his buzzer and I will come back to you," she said and quietly left the room. I took up my position at his bedside and reached out for his hand. I chatted away as if he could hear me. I told him all my news, about his sisters and about Alison's baby. To me he didn't look any different. Sharon Skelton kept popping her head round the door and I drank endless cups of tea and still there was no change. The time dragged by and I was beginning to feel very downhearted and tired. I looked at my watch and it was five o'clock. I had been here all day. Jed still looked the same and Sharon Skelton suggested I should go home. "We will send for you if there is any change," she said, and apologised for raising my hopes. "It's alright," I said as I reluctantly left the room, "I am grateful you are taking good care of Jed." I caught the bus home and let myself into the house. Steven was not home and I suddenly realised I hadn't eaten all day, just endless cups of tea. I decided to make myself an omelette but I didn't feel very hungry. I was just about to break the egg into the bowl when the phone rang. I picked up the receiver and said, "Hello." It was Steven saying he was delayed at the office. He could tell by my voice there was something wrong. I explained what had happened and I was near to tears. "Don't worry darling," he said, "I will be home as quickly as I can and I will look after you." I returned to the kitchen and made my omelette but I had a struggle trying to eat it. I felt so disillusioned. Steven arrived home half an hour later and came over to the sink where I was clearing up. He put his arms around my shoulders and said, "Come on love try to cheer up." I turned round towards him and snuggled up close and he held me tight. This was all I needed.

The days went by and nothing seemed to change. I went straight to the hospital from school everyday and Jed had not made any improvement. In fact he looked more fragile than ever and I began to think he was never going to get better. I spoke to the doctor about him but he didn't give me much hope. I was feeling so depressed, but Steven was a tower of strength. My daughters helped me and I know the toll was beginning to affect their lives, but life had to go on and we tried to make the best of things. I even found myself praying that if he was going to die, I hoped the dear Lord would take him, as I couldn't bear to see him gradually getting weaker.

It was now six weeks since the pit disaster and my Jed was the only one left in hospital. I would sit by his side and hold his hand and talk to him about the same old things over and over again. I talked of his childhood, his sisters, and most of all about his lovely dad who he had never known. I willed him to get better and his sisters often joined me in my stories. Sally always seemed to be the brightest and she would pretend to shout at him and tell him it was time he pulled himself together and come back to us. I would pretend to tell her off but one evening she was having her usual banter with him when suddenly he opened his eyes. His hand moved up towards his face and I quickly jumped out of my seat and Sally and I leaned over to be near him. "Press the buzzer quick," I said to Sally as I looked at Jed's face. His eyes flickered and he seemed to be trying to focus. Sally pressed the buzzer and opened the door to let in Sharon Skelton. "He's opened his eyes," she cried. Sharon was quickly by my side as she felt for Jed's pulse. Jed's eyes remained open and he was blinking in despair. Sharon spoke softly to him. "Can you hear me Jed?" she questioned. A faint sound came from Jed's lips and he moved his head as if to find comfort. I couldn't speak, I was so overwhelmed. Sally put her arm around my shoulder. "Oh! mum isn't this just wonderful," she said. I felt myself shaking and Sharon Skelton quickly sat me down. I'll get the doctor straight away," she said, "I will send in Nurse Kelly." She left the room and in came Nurse Kelly. "This is what we needed," she said as she moved over to my Jed's side. I couldn't take my eyes off him, he was still trying to mutter something, and his eyes kept opening. His right arm was reaching up to his face and I felt in awe. Sally was squeezing my hand and tears rolled down our cheeks.

Suddenly the door flew open and in dashed Dr Osborne followed by Sister Skelton. "Can you leave us for a few minutes," he said briskly, "I want to examine your son." Reluctantly we left the room and retired to the waiting room. Sally sat and held my hand. "Mum this is what we have been praying for," she said and I was too upset to speak. After what seemed an eternity, but was probably only half an hour, we were called back into Jed's room. Dr Osborne was waiting for us and I could tell by the look on his face that the news of Jed was good. "I am so happy for you," he said, "you will be pleased to know that your son is gradually coming out of his coma." I could have put my arms around him but all I could do was stand and cry. He moved over to me and held my arm. "Thank you so much," I managed to whisper as I sobbed till I thought my heart would break. "Come on now," said the doctor, "this won't do, there is still a long way to go, and you need to be strong. Jed will need all the help you can give him so let's have no more tears." "I will do my best," I answered, and Dr Osborne left the room.

Chapter 28

The weeks passed by and gradually my precious son came back to me. His scars were healing and he was at last aware of the world around him. I would go to the hospital and spend so much time talking to him and now he was able to answer me. Then the day came when I was told he could come home. I sorted out a bedroom for him and he came back to our house. He was very weak and it took a while for him to walk again, but once I got him home I was able to make a fuss of him. Bernice Kelly rang and asked if she could come to see him. This little bright-eyed Irish nurse was such a blessing to us. Her and Jed seemed to get along fine and it was lovely to have her around. Steven spent endless hours with him and gradually the time came for us to talk of his future. I left him to make the decision as to what he wanted to do with his life, and, apart from a few scars for which he still needed treatment he seemed pretty much back to normal. He decide he would go back to live at Colliery Terrace with his sisters and he was invited to spend some time at a rehabilitation centre on the East Coast. As he left I said a quiet prayer of thanks for my son's recovery.

The house seemed very strange without him and we went to see him at the nursing home where he was staying. We found this lovely place overlooking the sea and a much quieter and calmer Jed enjoying relaxing with the help of the people around him. He was there for two months and during this time I became a Grandma. Alison's baby was born at the beginning of November, a little girl, Jennifer Ann. I was so excited, Alison and David were over the moon. Jed came back home and it was decided he would go on a training course to become an electrician, and, although he was somewhat more subdued since the accident, I could still sense the same Jed sparkling with life.

Steven and I went over to see my new granddaughter and she was gorgeous. Alison handed her to me and said to Steven, "Come on Granddad you must nurse her." Steven took the baby from me and looked at her so adoringly, he looked a real professional although he had never had anything to do with babies before. We spent a lovely weekend with them and it was agreed they would all spend Christmas with us.

It was lovely to have life back to normal once again. I was doing well in my job. The school was getting excellent results and Steven's business was flourishing. I felt I had neglected my daughters but they assured me they were alright. Joanne was now married and still working in Bristol. I would have liked to have seen more of her and her husband, but they were always busy. She was working on the children's ward at one of the main hospitals and she rang me every week and filled me in with the stories of the children she cared for. Some were happy stories about the children who overcame some terrible life threatening illnesses and some of the poor children who didn't make it. Yes, she was a very devoted doctor and I felt very proud of her. Sally was busy planning her wedding for early spring and Angela was getting engaged to Andy at Christmas. Natalie had her own business in town and worked very hard. I always heard stories about how much better her clients felt when they had visited her beauty parlour for either a facial or a massage. She had one or two boyfriends but didn't seem ready to settle down. Jed seemed to be getting better every day and was attending the local college. He and Bernice had become a couple and were very happy together. The pit was still working and the miners seemed to have a better life style with better pay and conditions but, of course, it was still a very hazardous job.

My mother and stepfather were now getting old, but I still saw them every week. My stepbrother, Edward was now working his own smallholding and was married with three young children, so he was always busy.

As Christmas approached, Steven suggested we had a big family get together and everyone should come to our house. I knew it would be hectic but what a great way to celebrate Jed's recovery. So everyone was invited and I didn't forget my lovely friend, Mary. I knew she was very frail but I just hoped she would be well enough to travel. Steven suggested travelling across and accompanying her back to our house.

I spent hours shopping and preparing for the great celebration. Steven's parents said they would join us and Jed asked if he could bring Bernice. Although she was working through part of Christmas, she would be able to spend some of the time with us. I was so pleased as to how their relationship was progressing, she had a calming influence on Jed, and they seemed very happy together. Joanne and Simon said they would be able to make it. She had already told us they were now expecting their first baby. Little Jennifer Ann was now a lovely baby and Alison and David said they would be able to come to us. I thought this would be a good opportunity to spoil my granddaughter.

When I broke up for the Christmas holidays I really put my back into getting everything ready and Steven set off for Ireland to fetch Mary. When I saw the car arrive in our drive, I couldn't get out of the house quick enough. I helped Mary out of the car and held her in my arms. Although she was now in her late eighties, she had not lost any of her sparkle. "Oh! Mary, I am so happy to see you," I said as I wiped the tears from my eyes, but these were tears of joy, not tears of tragedy like the ones we had shared together so many times through the years.

I helped her into the house and sat her on the kitchen chair whilst I put the kettle on. "How are you?" I questioned. "I'll be feeling fine," she answered in her lovely lilting voice, "it's so good to be here."

So my life now felt complete, and, as I drew the curtains that night I saw the snow beginning to fall, and I thanked God for all my blessings.

The
Wheels
Turn